HONOUR

HONOUR

ACHIEVING JUSTICE
FOR BANAZ MAHMOD

CAROLINE GOODE

ONEWORLD

A Oneworld Book

First published by Oneworld Publications Ltd, 2020

ISBN 978-1-78607-545-1
eISBN 978-1-78607-546-8

Typeset by Hewer Text UK Ltd, Edinburgh
Printed and bound in Great Britain by Clays Ltd, Elcograf S.p.A.

This is a work of non-fiction, reconstructed from court records and
the author's memory. Although reasonable efforts have been made
to ensure that the information given is accurate, the publisher
assumes no responsibility in the case of an inadvertent error.

Oneworld Publications Ltd
10 Bloomsbury Street, London, WC1B 3SR, England
3754 Pleasant Ave, Suite 100, Minneapolis, MN 55409, USA

Stay up to date with the latest books,
special offers, and exclusive content from
Oneworld with our newsletter

Sign up on our website
oneworld-publications.com

MIX
Paper from
responsible sources
FSC® C018072

CONTENTS

Prologue   vii

PART ONE: FINDING BANAZ
Missing   3
Lines of Inquiry   17
Banaz Speaks   31
Omerta   45
Our Girl   61
The Timeline   71
Finding Banaz   83
A String of Beads   99
Case for the Prosecution   109
The Funeral   121

PART TWO: JUSTICE FOR BANAZ
The Prosecution   127
The Defence   141
Reasonable Doubt   155
The Verdict   165

Loose Ends   177
Erbil   187
The Knot   197
The Final Hearing   211
The Last Word   223

Acknowledgements   227

PROLOGUE

Most murder investigations start with a dead body. The investigation is almost formulaic. The crime scene is examined and lines of enquiry are developed. A post-mortem examination takes place which normally gives you a cause of death. Witnesses are interviewed, CCTV and telecommunications data examined, so that by the time you are searching addresses you know at least what you are looking for.

Each homicide team in London – there were twenty-four in 2005 – was led by a detective chief inspector or DCI. He (there were no female DCIs at that time) oversaw either two or three detective inspectors, five detective sergeants, a dozen or so detective constables and a number of civilian support staff. That's what it said on paper, anyway.

The fact that I found myself in charge of Team 16 on the world-famous Metropolitan Police Homicide and Serious Crime Command was a stroke of great good fortune. Just before Banaz Mahmod went missing, my DCI handed in his notice. Out of the three of us detective inspectors on Team

16, one was brand new and the other was offered a job elsewhere. I soon found myself acting DCI by default.

At any one time, three out of the twenty-four teams are "on call", covering the initial response to all murders across London. Another team might then take over an investigation based on their capacity. That is known as being "in the frame", a legacy from the days when a team's details were literally entered into a wooden frame at Scotland Yard. Each team would already be dealing with between ten and fifteen murders at various stages of investigation. But nobody likes handing jobs over to another team. The honest truth is that homicide investigation work is absolutely fascinating. Sad – yes. Horrifying even, but interesting and rewarding like nothing else I have ever experienced.

When Banaz went missing, Team 16 were on call, with me at the helm for the first time, and I was determined to prove myself. As the saying goes, "be careful what you wish for". My first case as DCI did not start with a body. There was no post-mortem, not even a crime scene. Everything about the investigation was upside down, it was like working in reverse. We didn't know who or what we were looking for. Unlike most murders, we didn't even know if this one had happened.

PART ONE

FINDING BANAZ

MISSING

Lewisham, South London, January 2006

The call almost always comes in the wee small hours, when you are awakened from a deep sleep by the mobile ringing. You stand there in the freezing cold, trying to keep your voice down so you don't wake the family, trying to clear your head enough to take in the vital information and planning, even while you are still taking in the details, what needs to be done, when and by whom.

Police refer to the initial response to any critical incident as the "golden hour". Those first crucial minutes after a crime has been reported might be your only opportunity to gather vital evidence, to seize exhibits and to trace witnesses and suspects. If you mess it up at the beginning, it is very difficult, sometimes impossible, to recover it later. There is nothing quite like it for focussing the mind.

The call that sparked this investigation, however, didn't happen like that. It came late one January afternoon from a detective inspector (DI) based at Merton. He was calling the Homicide Command for advice as he was worried about one of his missing persons.

A missing-persons investigation can be difficult to get right. With some cases, like missing children, you know you have to throw everything you have at it in order to recover the child as quickly as possible. If a child has been abducted, statistics show that there is only a small time window before the child is killed.

With missing adults, however, it is far more difficult. Adults go missing for all sorts of reasons – maybe because they want to, maybe because they haven't thought to tell someone where they are. They have greater means and motive to go missing than children and, on the whole, are less vulnerable. For that reason, far fewer police resources are expended on investigating missing adults unless there are very obvious aggravating factors.

The story told to me by the local DI was this: he was investigating the disappearance of a young Kurdish woman by the name of Banaz Mahmod. Banaz had been the subject of an arranged marriage, but had left her husband in July the previous year due to physical and sexual abuse, returning to live with her parents in south London. She had subsequently started a relationship with another man, Rahmat Suleimani, and it was he who was now reporting her missing.

Rahmat had explained that for a Kurdish woman to leave her husband brought shame on the whole community and that it was common for the woman to be killed by her family in order to restore their honour. He claimed that Banaz's uncle, Ari Mahmod, had threatened to kill both him and Banaz, and had in fact already made attempts on both of their lives.

Police records confirmed that eight weeks earlier, Banaz had indeed reported that her uncle Ari had threatened to kill her. Uniformed police officers had visited Banaz's address and spoken to her parents, who were absolutely adamant that they did not want to report her as a missing person. They told police they were very liberal parents. Their daughters were free to come and go as they pleased and frequently stayed out overnight. With that, the police had withdrawn from the property. If the parents were happy, surely there was no cause for concern?

But Rahmat was persistent. He insisted that the parents were lying. Nothing could be further from the truth, he claimed: the daughters were virtually prisoners in their own home. The detective inspector and I agreed that there was enough to make us concerned for Banaz's welfare.

The Homicide Command in those days were mandated to take on other serious crime at their discretion. Successive swingeing government cut-backs had resulted in resources for local police stations being absolutely squeezed dry to the point where it was a struggle to investigate even the most basic offences. The fact that their results were as good as they were was a tribute to the commitment of the men and women who made the system work. But an investigation such as a high-risk missing person, particularly one with multiple suspects, would effectively wipe out a borough's investigative and analytical resources.

The DI was fully aware that without proof that Banaz was dead, the chances of the Homicide Command taking on the job were pretty minimal. He was just doing the responsible thing and touching base to see if there was anything I could suggest that he hadn't already thought of, two heads being better than one and all that. But I had been in his position, having spent three years as a DI in Lambeth. I knew just what it was like to cope with the onslaught, the non-stop tide of major crime, all the rapes, robberies and assaults, each with its potential for complaints and community dissatisfaction.

I offered him a compromise. Together we came up with an investigative strategy which he would manage with his own resources over the next twenty-four hours. If, after all the basic enquiries were exhausted, there was still no sign of Banaz, I would take the investigation off his hands.

The plan was to treat Rahmat and Banaz's parents and uncle as significant witnesses at that stage. We had insufficient information to treat them as suspects. I wanted thorough, comprehensive searches at Banaz's home address, Rahmat's address, Uncle Ari's address and Banaz's grandmother's address. Every loft, basement and outbuilding needed to be searched and I wanted any phones, computers, diaries, bank statements, travel cards – absolutely anything from which we could glean information about Banaz's lifestyle and movements.

I wanted those closest to her to commit to an account, both to provide me with all the relevant information and so I could get a feel for those involved, Rahmat included. At that stage, I didn't know what his involvement or motivation was. After all, he wouldn't be the first young man to murder his girlfriend and then report her missing.

The detective inspector and I agreed to speak again in twenty-four hours. The date was 26 January 2006 and my life was just about to change.

While the local officers went off to carry out their enquiries on the Banaz case, life went on as normal for us on the Homicide Command. It was a frenetic on-call week and the calls came in thick and fast. A man had fallen from a tower block and it was alleged he had been pushed. A woman had been found dead in a burning flat and it was considered suspicious. One man had been found dead in his bath.

Another was in hospital with life-threatening stab injuries. A woman had died of a drug overdose and there was an allegation a third party had administered the drugs. Somebody else had died in hospital and it was alleged that a relative had "euthanised" them. And so it went on. We were doing the usual balancing act: attending crime scenes, going to post-mortem examinations and making numerous enquiries in addition to managing another dozen or so live murder inquiries.

The twenty-four hours I had agreed with the local DI passed in the blink of an eye. He called me back in the late afternoon to tell me that he had completed all of our agreed actions and there was still no trace of Banaz. Without further ado, my fellow DI Rick Murphy and I rallied our team together and headed off from our base in Lewisham, south east London, to Wimbledon police station in the south west.

Rick Murphy was an experienced detective, a tenacious, gritty investigator and nobody's fool. We had not yet had the opportunity to work together as I had just returned from a lengthy trial at the Old Bailey, but it is fair to say we got on like a house on fire right from the get-go. He was a few years younger than me, but we were both outspoken Londoners, both Spurs supporters (God help us), and we both gave body and soul for The Job. I loved his sense of humour and hunger for work.

Over at Wimbledon, the tiny briefing room was packed to capacity with homicide detectives and local officers who had been managing the inquiry thus far. There was the palpable sense of heightened anticipation that always comes with taking over a new investigation. Thirty notebooks opened and detectives started scribbling furiously as the local officers told us what they knew.

Banaz Mahmod was a nineteen-year-old woman of Iraqi Kurdish origin. She had come to the UK with her family when she was ten, fleeing from Saddam Hussein's regime. She had four sisters and an older brother. Banaz had attended local schools until the age of sixteen, when she married a man called Ali Abass Homar. In July 2005, after only two years of marriage, Banaz left her husband and moved back in with her parents.

Records suggested that Banaz had repeatedly come into contact with the police, both during her relationship with her husband and after. She had reported that she had been repeatedly raped and beaten by her husband. As well as reporting that her uncle had threatened to kill her and Rahmat, she had also told the police her father had attempted to kill her on New Year's Eve. She even presented the police with a list of those she thought wished her harm. Rahmat, too, had come to the police to inform them of an attempt on his life at the hands of several on that list.

On 24 January 2006, the day before Rahmat reported her missing, Banaz had another appointment with the police, but she never showed up. We would come to wonder what more it would have taken for her to make the desperate nature of her situation clear to the police.

In addition to tracing all of the police reports, the local police had also interviewed Banaz's father, Mahmod Babakir Mahmod, her mother, Behya, and her uncle Ari as significant witnesses.

Mahmod was the eldest of four brothers. Neither he nor his wife worked. They lived in a modest semi-detached house at 225 Morden Road, Morden, a suburb of south west

London. Also living at home were his only son and his youngest daughter, then aged sixteen. Two more daughters were
married and living elsewhere. Another daughter was believed
to be estranged from the family, but little was known about
her. All of them would later become hugely relevant to the
inquiry.

In the interview, Mahmod described Ali Abass Homar as
the "David Beckham" of husbands. He was perfect husband
material, a man they knew from Qaladiza, the small town
where they used to live in Kurdistan. Mahmod said he was
aware that there had been "minor" problems in Banaz's
marriage, but provided no details. Banaz left Ali in 2005 and
one month later said she was in love with another man.
Mahmod had met Rahmat and was OK about their relationship. His daughters were free to come and go as they pleased
and it was not unusual for Banaz to stay out for a day or two.
When asked about the events of New Year's Eve, he described
his daughter as a foolish young woman experimenting with
alcohol. He had last seen Banaz on the night of 23 January.
He was aware that she was going to the police the following
day but had no idea what for. This account of his last sighting
of Banaz was noted to differ from one that he had given to
another officer, to whom he had stated that he saw Banaz on
the morning of the 24th when she was wearing blue jeans
and a dark top. Mahmod also claimed to be estranged from
his younger brother, Ari, and said they had barely spoken to
each other for a long time.

Ari Mahmod was far wealthier than his older brother,
being the owner of several businesses. At that time, it was
known that he owned a couple of supermarkets and was also
renovating a large property on Wandsworth Road in South
Lambeth, which he was converting into flats. Ari lived in a

large house in Mitcham, not far from Morden, with his wife, two daughters and one son. His account was that he was aware that Banaz had separated from her husband but was not sure of their legal status. Like his brother, Ari held Ali Abass Homar in high regard. He stated that he had been visited by Ali and his brother back in July or August. Ali had told Ari about his separation from Banaz, and Ari had asked what he might do to help. Ari claimed not to know where the Homar brothers lived. He said that he had last spoken to the brothers two to three months before, when Ali had wanted his assistance to get some property back from Banaz. Ari had advised him to go through Mahmod.

Ari claimed he was neither on good nor bad terms with his brother, Mahmod, though he had not visited him for eight months. But he also said that Mahmod had called on him on the evening of 25 January, the day Banaz was reported missing. Ari had been at the building site on Wandsworth Road. He was standing outside when Mahmod just turned up, unannounced. The brothers went into the back garden where they stood by a bonfire and chatted about renovation, he said.

I could see the team exchanging glances when this was mentioned. The week before, we had dealt with a domestic murder where an Asian man had killed his wife and disposed of her remains by burning them in a bonfire. We made a mental note to examine the remains of the fire, hoping this wasn't another such grisly incident.

Ari was asked about the events of 2 December, the date on which Banaz alleged he had threatened to kill her and Rahmat. The way Ari told it was this: On 1 December he went to collect his new son-in-law from the airport. To welcome him into the country, he invited the men of the family over to his house. Present at this meeting were his two youngest brothers, a cousin and two men named Mohammed Saleh Ali and Mohammed Hama. Those last two were already on the list that Banaz had drawn up, together with a third man called Omar Hussain. When asked whether Banaz had been discussed at this meeting, Ari stated that she had cropped up in conversation, and that they all agreed how happy they were for her that she was in another relationship. Ari was aware that Banaz had been photographed kissing Rahmat as he had heard gossip to that effect.

Banaz's mother, Behya, presented herself as both unwell and unworldly. She had to ask her husband's permission before speaking to us. Speaking through an interpreter, she said that Banaz, having been seen kissing Rahmat, told her that she had been photographed and threatened. When asked about Ari's death threat, Behya stated that she remembered getting a telephone call from Ari, but really couldn't remember whether Ari had threatened to kill Banaz or not. When pressed on the subject, she claimed to be feeling unwell. It was the opinion of the interviewing officer that the illness was put on, an excuse not to answer questions.

Behya also claimed to have last seen Banaz on the morning of 24 January. She said she saw Banaz sleeping on the living room floor. This is where Banaz slept, there being no room for her elsewhere. She described her as naked apart from a pair of shorts, which differed from both of the accounts given by Banaz's father. She knew Banaz was due at the police station that day, but did not know what for. She brought her daughter a cup of tea and told her, "Don't forget you have an appointment at the police station." The fact that both she and Mahmod knew about that appointment would later become highly significant. She and Mahmod had then taken their youngest daughter to school at about 08:30. They had gone shopping together and returned home at about 10:30, at which time Banaz was no longer there. The bedding was all neatly packed away. Behya had not considered that anything was amiss.

So, there it was. Our job was now to unravel the confused story and find this woman who had reported her own murder and then gone missing. Even at that early stage we had four differing accounts and numerous criminal allegations, as well as multiple potential suspects, witnesses and crime scenes.

We sent the team away to get food and drink – you learn early to eat while you can in situations such as this, as you don't know when the next opportunity will arise. Rick and I discussed the case with the detective sergeant to determine our next course of action.

"Blimey," said Rick. "This is a proper 'ead scratcher, innit?"

The first thing I had to decide was what it was I was dealing with. Was this a missing-persons inquiry? Was Banaz being held against her will somewhere, or in hiding? Or was she already dead? Was this, in fact, already a murder case? There were a number of hypotheses that presented themselves:

1. Banaz was missing of her own volition as the result of a disagreement with the family.
2. Banaz was missing of her own volition as the result of a disagreement with her boyfriend Rahmat and he was using the police to track her down.
3. Banaz was being held against her will by or on behalf of the family.

4. Banaz had been murdered by the family.
5. Banaz had been murdered by Rahmat.
6. Banaz had been murdered by persons unknown.
7. Banaz had come to harm in non-suspicious circumstances and was unable to make contact.

We turned over what little information we had in front of us. It did not seem as though Banaz had left of her own volition. Most of her belongings were still at her parents' address. Her passport was there, as were most of her clothes. Her handbag and mobile phone were missing, but no money had been taken from her bank account and there was no usage on her phone. It had been used at just past midnight on the night of the 23rd to check the credit balance, and analysis of the cell towers showed that this would have been in the area of her home address. It was the lack of use of the mobile that gave us most concern, because this was clearly a young woman who lived on her phone.

Initial analysis of Rahmat's mobile revealed a whole raft of text messages from Banaz. The texts painted a picture of a couple in a loving relationship. It also showed that, contrary to her parents' claims, they did not approve of the relationship and it was going on in secret against their wishes. The texts also showed that Banaz was strictly controlled by her father. On one occasion, she told Rahmat, she had had to pretend she was going to buy "period towels", simply to get away from Mahmod for long enough to send a text.

Banaz texted Rahmat every day. It was the first thing she did every morning as she opened her eyes. On 7 January she had sent him a message which said, "I love you Rahmat, my life, you are my inspiration for getting up every day. You are the reason I am living today." On 23 January her message read, "Jus be careful, Rahmat, gian, cus I dnt fink I cud live a second widout u. I love you so much xxxxx". (*Gian* is a term of endearment, meaning "my heart".) The first morning that she didn't send him a message was the 24th.

Without positive proof that she was already dead, we worked on the proposition that she was still alive, being held against her will somewhere, and from that moment it became a race against time to find her before some further harm befell her. My priorities were therefore to find and recover Banaz, alive if possible, and if not, to recover her body and, either way, to bring her offenders to justice. No slow burn this, no measured, covert operation to trace her without showing our hand. We were past that stage already. Houses had been searched, witnesses interviewed. We had to act quickly.

We called the team back to brief them on our decision and allocate core roles.

I had known Detective Sergeant Andy Craig, or Craigy as he is better known, since the early 1980s. We had both served at Carter Street, a tough patch in Walworth, south east London, where you quickly found out who could be relied upon. As a young PC, Craigy had been highly energetic and enthusiastic. A good footballer, he had ginger hair cut into the wedge style popular in the day. He was an excellent copper with a natural gift for talking to people – not a skill that can be taught but one of the best skills a police officer can possess. I don't know his secret, but I know you can put him in a room with a suspect who wants to rip your head off your shoulders and half an hour later he'll have agreed to play in a friendly football match.

Twenty years on, Craigy might have been a bit slower on the pitch and his hair might have receded a bit, but pretty much nothing else had changed. By the time we took over the Banaz investigation, we had worked together at a number of postings. We each liked the way the other worked and I always sought him out for recruitment. We had already worked on several murders together and in my opinion, he had been pivotal in solving all of them. I loved him like the little brother I never had. He called me Smudger – an old Carter Street nickname – or Mum. Everyone knew I detested being called ma'am, and "Mum" was a way of having a dig at that and taking the mickey out of me for being older than the rest of the team. Thanks to Craigy, I soon had e-mails from various lads on the team signing off as Son #5 or Son #6.

Craigy's role was to run the intelligence team. An all-female team, it consisted of one detective constable, three researchers and our brand new intelligence analyst, Keilly McIntyre. That intel team were fantastic, every one of them willing and diligent.

The other detective sergeant with a core role in the investigation was Stuart Reeves. Stuart, AKA Big Stu, was a gentle giant, weighing in at 22 stone. He was a relative newcomer to the team, having come to us on promotion from another Lewisham homicide team, but he had already made a huge impression. He was unfailingly genial, good natured and highly intelligent. Apart from being hard working and good at his job, he was just so damned likeable – I have still never met a single person who didn't love Stuart.

We told the team that we were going to conduct a major search-and-arrest operation, hitting numerous addresses simultaneously in the early hours of the following morning. Any address where Banaz could conceivably be was on the list. The logistical difficulties were obvious from the outset. With multiple addresses to search and multiple suspects, this inquiry was going to be massively resource intensive. Even on that first night we had a dozen suspects. Officers worked through the night, obtaining search warrants, researching addresses and suspects, assembling briefing packages, exhibit packages, enforcers and vehicles, and reserving cells. With no time to lose, we begged, borrowed and stole officers from everywhere we could think of: Merton Borough, Lambeth Borough, the Territorial Support Group, other murder teams, dog handlers, traffic police, even officers from the West Midlands and Yorkshire constabularies – anyone who could be spared.

There was something else worrying me. An intelligence report showed that Banaz's youngest sister was being followed to and from school by Kurdish men. One of the men was believed to be the owner of a Mediterranean grocery shop near Morden Underground station. That was where Banaz and Rahmat had been seen kissing. Was this man significant? Why were people following the little sister? She hadn't done anything wrong that we were aware of. Was she also at risk?

Meanwhile, our analyst Keilly was already at work trying to trace Banaz's husband, Ali Abass Homar. A live trace on his mobile phone showed he was not at his home address in Sheffield. Keilly advised me that the data showed he was travelling across the Pennines and had stopped on Saddleworth Moor. In my mind's eye, I saw the black and white photo of Keith Bennett, the little lad murdered by Myra Hindley and Ian Brady, buried up there on the moors when I was a kid and never found. Please, God, I prayed, don't let that have happened to Banaz.

That night was the first of many sleepless nights.

LINES OF INQUIRY

We now began to piece a timeline together, which would be vital to establishing what had really happened.

On 4 December 2005, Banaz attended Wimbledon police station to report that her uncle Ari had threatened to kill her and Rahmat. She said men had been following her in the street and had photographed her and Rahmat kissing near Morden station. Those men informed Ari, who in turn called her mother on the landline and told her that Banaz and Rahmat would both be killed for bringing shame on the family.

On 12 December, Banaz delivered a letter to Wimbledon police station, naming some of the people that she had heard were going to kill her. In his statement to police, Rahmat stated that he thought it was one of Ari's daughters who had passed on this information to Banaz, but he didn't know for certain. He also told detectives that Banaz's own father had tried to kill her on New Year's Eve.

It was on New Year's Eve, we discovered, that Banaz stumbled into a café and collapsed on the floor. She repeatedly told staff in the café that her father had tried to kill her at her grandmother's house and that she had smashed a neighbour's window in order to get help. A police officer recorded the incident as criminal damage to the window.

On 22 January 2006, there was an attempt to kidnap and murder Rahmat. He had been visiting a friend in Hounslow, on the western outskirts of London, at the time. As he left the house with a couple of friends, a Ford Focus pulled up next to him. Inside were the three Kurdish men who had been named in Banaz's letter to the police, along with a fourth he didn't recognise. Having unsuccessfully tried to force Rahmat into the car, the men told him, "OK, we cannot take you now but we are going to kill you and we are going to kill Banaz. You cannot carry on doing what you are doing. You are not English. You are Kurdish and Muslim and you are going to die." Rahmat phoned Banaz to warn her and both were so worried that they each went to a separate police station to seek help.

On 28 January, the day following our briefing in Wimbledon, we had both Ari and Mahmod arrested. We had enough to change their status from persons of interest to suspects. There was still no activity on Banaz's bank account or phone; Banaz's texts to Rahmat showed that the relationship was disapproved of; Ari had confirmed a meeting had taken place in his home which had been attended by other suspects; we knew about the attempt on Banaz's life; we knew that Banaz's youngest sister was also being followed.

I resisted the urge to interview Ari myself, much as I wanted to. When you are the senior investigating officer, you have to discipline yourself sometimes not to stray too much into tactical work, so that you can keep the big picture in mind. I've never been one for standing back and I found it hard. Part of me wanted to see how Ari would react to having a female in a position of power over him but I also didn't want to give him any excuses not to talk.

Andy Craig got the pleasure of interviewing Ari at Sutton police station. Ari's attitude was so extraordinary that we took the decision to video-record the interview. The difference in his attitude from being a significant witness to being a suspect was marked. No longer courteous, he now radiated hatred and arrogance, even malevolence. It was easy to see why people in his community feared him – especially girls. His tone was contemptuous, sneering, refusing even to acknowledge the right of the interviewer to ask him questions. It was fascinating.

Stuart Reeves interviewed Mahmod, who was less menacing but no more helpful. Neither answered any of the questions put to them in interview and they were released on bail. The surveillance team who followed their shared taxi home said they were clearly having a massive altercation. I bet they were – things were not going according to plan.

We searched numerous addresses all over the country, hunting for the three men who had been named on Banaz's list: Omar Hussain, Mohammed Ali and Mohammed Hama. None were at their home addresses. At Mohammed Ali's address in Northbourne Road, Brixton, the only person present was a man we hadn't come across before named Sardar Sharif Mahmod, who claimed to be no relation to our Mahmods. He was not deemed relevant to the investigation at that time. Instead we tried the notorious local cab firm where Mohammed Ali was known to work, but he hadn't been seen there for days. We found out that both he and Mohammed Hama also worked part time in Electric Avenue,

Brixton, as butchers and pondered the possibility that Banaz might have been dismembered at one of the premises.

Up in Birmingham, we found Omar Hussain's vehicle outside his address, but no sign of our suspect. Rahmat had heard a rumour that Omar had been arrested but no trace could be found of him in the system. We circulated the three of them as wanted and put out an "all ports" warning to stop them fleeing. Almost immediately we were contacted by the police in Stranraer, in south west Scotland. Omar Hussain had passed through there just the day before, they said. At first, I thought it must be a mistake. As far as I knew, Omar had no connection to Scotland.

I called the officer in Scotland. It transpired that a couple of days after Banaz's disappearance, Omar had been arrested in Birmingham for a public order offence. He had apparently become involved in a fight and had then been verbally abusive towards a police officer. Once he was in custody, it was discovered that he was wanted for failing to appear in court in Scotland for a driving offence and he was transferred up there. All pretty low-level stuff, but it proved where he was on certain days and times. When you have little to go on in the way of evidence, you are grateful for whatever you can get. What we weren't grateful for, though, was the fact that he had just skipped the country.

A number of other Kurdish men were arrested, including those who had allegedly photographed Rahmat and Banaz kissing. They lied about just about everything. One young man known as Kherat was named by Banaz in her letter. He denied his own name, even when it was pointed out that his brother had identified him. He was related to Ari's wife but claimed to have no relationship with Ari and never to have seen Banaz. He denied being at the meeting at Ari's house on

2 December, despite being named by several others as having been there. He denied ever calling Ari in relation to Banaz, too, but his phone data suggested otherwise.

At another address, several men jumped out of a window but were detained and arrested. Virtually all were related to each other and to the Mahmod family somehow. One had lived with Omar Hussain but denied knowing him. He firstly claimed never to have heard of Banaz but later said he was a friend of her father and had seen her the previous year. Intelligence suggested this man had been following Banaz's sister to and from school, something he also denied. This man lived at the grocery shop in Morden where Banaz and Rahmat had been seen kissing, and he was also a cousin of Banaz's eldest sister's husband. It was becoming obvious how inter-related and entangled the group were, but who was respons-ible for what was another matter. It was like trying to unravel a huge ball of string without being able to find the end.

Ali Abass Homar and his brother were both arrested at their address in Sheffield. Stuart Reeves started his interview with Ali by placing a photograph of Banaz on the table. Ali promptly turned it over. He didn't want to look at her. Every time Stuart asked him to look at the photo he would turn it face down on the table. Why was that? Was it relevant? Was there something in her eyes that stirred a vestige of guilt in him? We didn't know. Ali gave an account of his movements for the relevant time period, including the journey across the Pennines. He had been visiting a friend in Wrexham, in north east Wales, who had just got out of prison. If true, it would mean he had an alibi. The story would have to be checked out. Officers were sent to Sheffield and Wrexham.

At the same time, as a result of our missing persons appeal, a member of the public got in touch to say she had seen two Asian-looking men carrying something out of a parked car up on Saddleworth Moor. Possibly a carpet, she couldn't say. We duly dispatched an officer to search the area with locals.

Meanwhile, in Wimbledon, Detective Sergeant Richard Vandenburgh was in charge of the search at the home address of Banaz's grandmother, where Mahmod had allegedly attempted to murder Banaz on New Year's Eve. While Richard was there he met two of Banaz's cousins, Dana Amin and Hassan Mahmod. Dana was described as cocky, and was keen to show Richard the boot of his Lexus, which looked as though it had just been valeted. Neither of the cousins lived there, but they claimed to have been out together and come back there for the night.

I was unhappy with their account from the outset. Years of listening to people giving their accounts, true or false, means you are mentally tying up the ends without even realising you are doing it, listening for the falsehood, visualising, even as you are listening. It's not a skill, necessarily, just a habit. Sadly, Richard hadn't seized the vehicle at that stage, or got Dana to commit formally to his account, something we would later regret.

Rick Murphy and I barely saw each other in those first few days. We were just too busy. However hard I tried to keep the investigation structured, there weren't enough hours in the day. By day three, it almost felt like the inquiry was beginning to run away from me. I just about managed to grab hold of Rick to sit and talk over a cup of tea in the canteen for ten minutes. We reviewed our strategy, made sure we were on the same wavelength and got straight back to it.

Information was flooding into the inquiry almost too fast to keep up with. The cells were full, we had multiple suspect interviews going on simultaneously, searches ongoing, covert work happening; it was mental. In the early days, we held twice-daily meetings to ensure the whole team could keep abreast of the latest information and steer the inquiry in the right direction. The pace was intense. Nobody went home for days. All the normal missing-persons enquiries had to be carried out: refuges were contacted, witnesses sought, CCTV harvested, house-to-house enquiries conducted. Officers were snatching a couple of hours of sleep on the floor and nipping across the road to Marks and Spencer to buy new shirts and underwear. Our new analyst set up residence in the archive cupboard and didn't go home for weeks.

Other lines of inquiry involved looking into the mobile phones used by the suspects. Analysis of such data can be critical in a murder inquiry but it doesn't appear magically on a touchscreen like in the movies. Every single item of data has to be separately applied for and authorised. The claims by some that we live in a police state where everyone's data is routinely looked at by police and security services were not true in my experience. Privacy is taken very seriously. The results of the data applications arrive in dribs and drabs, some taking longer than others. When they do arrive, the data is in a raw format and has to be painstakingly analysed. Who are the phones attributable to? Where were the respective callers at the time the call was made, and what is the relevance? Can the usage by that person be corroborated any other way?

Because it all comes in at different times, you have an incomplete jigsaw that changes with every receipt of new information. I have a memory of sitting at my dining room table in the early hours of one sleepless night, writing on two

pieces of A3 paper sellotaped together, wading through pages
of raw data, trying to make sense of it all. That is the job of
specialist analysts, of course, but I just couldn't wait. Looking
at an old notebook I can see numerous questions I had written to myself: what was so-and-so doing there? Who is this
person Ari is talking to? Where was this call made from?
Who does this phone belong to?

Analysis of the communications data was the job of Keilly
McIntyre. Keilly was twenty-seven years old and new to
homicide work. An attractive blonde, with legs up to her
armpits, Keilly drew admiring glances wherever she went,
but she was definitely not just a pretty face. Within a couple
of weeks of starting, she was getting e-mails congratulating
her on the quality of her telephone applications. It wasn't
even her job to be writing them, she just absorbed work like
a sponge. The person whose job it was just couldn't keep up
with Keilly and she needed the data now.

She was also somewhat unorthodox. Anyone will tell you
that I have an extremely relaxed management style and don't
like to stand on ceremony, but Keilly took this to extremes.
She seemed to have no concept of protocol. She would often
bounce into my office to show me her latest revelation with a
cheery "Hiya, Cazza, guess what I've found." Her brain power
was incredible – there were times we had to ask her to slow
down when she was explaining her various hypotheses to us,
as we couldn't keep up. Unorthodox she might have been –
but she was bloody brilliant. In the early days we had very
little for her to go on, but she would soon come into her own.

Over the course of the first two weeks we searched forty-
seven addresses the length and breadth of the country,
arrested and interviewed in excess of thirty people, seized
more than twenty vehicles and over 300 mobile telephones,

plus numerous computers and items of correspondence. We took everything that could conceivably have led us to Banaz's whereabouts or evidence of people's involvement in her disappearance. Every car, every phone, every computer, every scrap of writing which could not be eliminated at the scene. The exhibits officer was working round the clock just trying to keep up with the volume of items. The key to solving this case was going to be either in finding Banaz or a crime scene or in proving communication between relevant people at relevant times. That may sound simple enough, but who were the relevant people and what were the relevant times?

Every single address was searched under forensic conditions and examined by a specialist crime scene manager (CSM), with particular care taken to avoid cross-contaminating forensic evidence from one scene to another. We only had a finite number of CSMs and had to husband our resources as best we could, but we were allocated a dedicated manager, Calvin Lawson, who was an absolute godsend. Calvin was meticulous, committed and innovative, equally as driven as the rest of the team. He was invaluable in co-ordinating the forensic response.

So many of our most promising leads were dead ends. In the back yard of Ari's property on Wandsworth Road was a coffin. (It later transpired that the property had formerly been an undertaker's.) We dug through the ashes of that bonfire looking for human remains. (Nothing.) We searched the butcher's shops in Brixton. (Lots of blood and dismembered bodies, none of them human.) None of the addresses was a crime scene and there was not a trace of Banaz anywhere.

On the first Friday a member of our team, DC Nick Stocking, searched Mahmod's allotment and found traces of

blood. Was this it, did we have a breakthrough? Rick and I
hot-footed it across London to Morden. We treated the area
as a crime scene and a specialist search team came down to
go through those allotments with a fine-toothed comb.
Nothing was found other than the blood, which later turned
out to come from an animal.

Blood was turning up in all sorts of places: in a van seized
from the Mediterranean grocery store; in the Mahmods'
bathroom; on what looked like an altar in the basement of
another address in Sheffield; there was a small amount on
the front seat of Dana Amin's Lexus; the boot lining of Ari's
car reacted to Luminol, a chemical used by forensic examin-
ers to find traces of blood which cannot be seen by the naked
eye. So much blood, but none of it Banaz's. We still didn't
know if she had died or whether blood was even relevant.

In conjunction with the searches and arrests, we deployed
covert policing methods against the main suspects. Almost
immediately, however, the number of suspects started to
mushroom so that trying to put parameters around who to
prioritise became a nightmare. Who to follow? Who to listen
to? Whose phones to look at first? Any one of these people
could have had her hidden away somewhere. And with every
application for covert work comes a mountain of paperwork.
The more intrusive you want to be, the greater the level of
justification and escalation required. We needed this information quickly; we were trying to find Banaz before they
killed her. Again and again I found myself briefing increasingly senior officers on the telephone, persuading them to
allow me to conduct various forms of surveillance.

While this was going on, Rahmat had been assigned a
family liaison officer, who had taken a fuller statement. It is
very rare for a witness to be able to provide every bit of

relevant information in their first statement. That is difficult even if the incident is a one-off event. But when you are trying to recall events that have taken place over months or even years, it is far harder. Rahmat seemed to be doing his best to help – he just didn't know what was relevant and what wasn't.

He told us that Mahmod had warned him to stay away from Banaz the previous October. They had sat together in a car and Mahmod had told him the relationship could not continue. According to Rahmat, Mahmod had told him that "his brother would never allow it". He described another meeting, this time after the attempt on Banaz's life on New Year's Eve. While the rest of the family were in a McDonald's, Mahmod and Rahmat had a meeting of their own. Rahmat described Mahmod kissing his hand, crying and saying he should never have listened to his brother Ari. The picture we were getting was of Ari being by far the dominant brother, even the head of the family, despite Mahmod being the eldest.

Among other things, Rahmat was asked about telephone calls. Without even the need to consult his phone data, Rahmat described how, after the attempt to abduct him in Hounslow, he had called Mahmod in a rage and demanded to know why he had sent men to kill him. Rahmat had also phoned Ari and Omar on the same night. Little details like that were to prove highly significant later in the investigation.

The family liaison officer explored Rahmat's relationship with the suspects. When a relative had given the list of possible abductors to Banaz and told her about the meeting at Ari's house, Banaz had warned Rahmat. She had no idea who these people were, but Rahmat recognised the names immediately. He had been a friend of theirs for years and had even lived with Omar Hussain in the past. All of them were asylum seekers who had come to the UK from Kurdistan, seeking a better life. Banaz's information had proved correct when those three men later tried to abduct him from Hounslow.

Rahmat was living with his aunt near Waterloo station. He told Craigy that she had arranged to meet the Mahmods for a talk. The Mahmods tried to persuade Rahmat's relatives that he should drop the case. His aunt was also getting calls from Kurdistan: "Tell Rahmat to drop the case or he will be killed." It was the first indication we had that the community were collaborating to derail the inquiry. It seemed that the attempt to abduct him hadn't been a one-off – this was something larger and more sustained. We were now getting seriously concerned for Rahmat's safety. Straight away we contacted Witness Protection, who came and spoke to Rahmat, but he was unwilling to join. He was still hoping, as we were, that Banaz would be found alive, that he could save her and life could go on as before.

The DCI who sat across the corridor from me called out to enquire what I had picked up. Everyone on the Homicide Command keeps abreast of everyone else's investigations. There are several reasons for this. Partly it's professional interest. Every murder investigation is a learning exercise and by keeping on top of everyone else's jobs, that learning gets shared and promulgated. Perhaps more than that, it is a smattering of healthy competition and of course Old Bill doing what comes naturally and being nosy.

I gave the DCI a very brief overview of what I knew. I told him there was a possibility this was a case of honour-based violence. Neither of us had dealt with it before, so it was going to be a real learning curve. As I was walking away, he shouted out that he had recently seen a presentation by a former senior investigating officer by the name of Brent Hyatt, who had investigated a so-called honour killing. He volunteered to give Brent a call and pass on my details, which I gratefully accepted.

Brent had investigated the killing in 2003 of Heshu Yones, a young Iraqi Kurdish woman murdered by father. He wanted to help in any way he could. He volunteered to conduct an appeal for witnesses at the Kurdish Cultural Centre near the Oval in south London. We gave him the photo of Banaz that the family had provided. She was a beautiful young woman, though heavily made-up in this photo.

Photographs later recovered from Rahmat's phone showed that she looked nothing like the photo the family had given us. When Brent made his enquiries at the Kurdish Cultural Centre, he was advised by people there that nobody in the Kurdish community would know her by the name Banaz Mahmod. She would be known as Banaz Mahmod Babakir Agha. So the family had provided us with both a photo and a name that nobody would recognise. Was this deliberate? If you wanted your daughter to be found, wouldn't you provide the very best information you could?

With every day that passed and every search that didn't result in finding Banaz, the outlook became more and more bleak. The longer someone is missing, the greater the likelihood that some harm has befallen them. We never even acknowledged between ourselves that she was probably dead, we just kept going. We never gave up hope of finding our girl alive. That expression – "our girl". We already thought of her in those terms.

BANAZ SPEAKS

Lewisham, January 2006

While the initial searches and arrests were taking place, another part of the team was responsible for gathering all of the available information and entering it into a computer system aptly named HOLMES (Home Office Large Major Enquiry System). Every scrap of information goes into the system, every statement, every description, every message, exhibit or photograph.

Our inquiry had now been allocated a name – Operation Baidland (the names are generated randomly, by computer). In charge of pulling all this data together was DC Jon "Wiggle" Weighill, a veteran of many years on the murder teams. Wiggle was what is known as a safe pair of hands: totally efficient, good at his job and loyal as the day is long. Admin is definitely not my strong point, but Wiggle made sure he always had my back and kept me on the straight and narrow.

In the early stages of every investigation the senior investigating officer (SIO) goes through a process of demystification, trying to make sense of the information. There is a saying in the world of criminal investigation: "ABC: Accept nothing, Believe nobody and Check everything." Never is that more true than in a murder case. There are literally hundreds, if not thousands, of pieces of information to take into account and each must be sifted for relevance and accuracy.

One might receive a statement from a witness. That statement would then be assessed. Does it make sense in its own right? Does it further the investigation or is it irrelevant? Does it support the other information coming in or is it contradictory? If the latter, is there an explanation? Which version, if either, is correct?

That is difficult enough when you have a solid frame of reference against which to measure your material. When a man is shot or stabbed, the facts are often relatively straightforward. CCTV shows this, the forensics show that. All witnesses differ slightly, but if one is completely at odds with the others you may consider what their motive is or whether they have misunderstood the situation.

In this case, it was very different. We had Rahmat telling us one story and numerous members of Banaz's family telling us something else. Normally the family are the people you can count on to tell you the truth, but here the family's stories weren't even consistent. This was a cultural issue about which I had no knowledge. Was I guilty of jumping to conclusions? Was I misjudging them? Why would so many people get involved in what seemed on the face of it such a trivial matter?

While every piece of information gets assessed, it is important for the SIO to decide on a leading hypothesis. This enables you to prioritise lines of inquiry and not waste time chasing down irrelevant trivia. One of the reasons for arriving at the hypothesis that Banaz had been harmed by her family was the fact that she had made a number of allegations to police. A priority line of inquiry, therefore, was to scrutinise all of those allegations in detail, in effect to reinvestigate them, and to do so with an open mind. Wiggle pulled together all of the relevant reports for me. The trail of Banaz's allegations made horrifying reading and I very soon began to realise that the police might have made some terrible mistakes. The more I read, the sicker I felt.

In September 2005, Banaz had made an allegation of multiple counts of rape and assault at the hands of her husband. She had been interviewed by a specially trained officer. The transcript of that interview was a tragic story in its own right.

Banaz married Ali Abass Homar when she was sixteen years old. She had only met him on one previous occasion, at a family barbecue on her father's allotment. The marriage had apparently been arranged by her uncle Ari. Ali was from Qaladiza, near Sulaymaniyah in Iraqi Kurdistan, not far from the border with Iran. It was the town that Banaz's own family came from and he was from the same tribe, the Mirawdaly.

According to Banaz's account, Ali was ten years older than her. He was illiterate and didn't speak English. He had only recently arrived in the UK from Kurdistan and, judging by Banaz's account, he was strongly adherent to the Kurdish culture and clearly felt he needed to keep his more educated, young, westernised bride in her place. She described him as "thinking like fifty years ago", repeatedly raping and beating her, and she described herself as being confused. "I didn't know if this was how it was supposed to be, either in my culture or here. I was only seventeen . . . It was as if I was his shoe and he could wear me whenever he felt like it." On one occasion, he gave her a beating because she called him by his

given name in front of a guest, which he felt was disrespectful. He threatened to stick a knife in her if she ever did it
again. On another occasion, he beat her because she couldn't
spell a word he asked her to spell. He punched her so hard
that her ears bled and so often that she was suffering from
memory loss. This was the man Mahmod had described as
"the David Beckham of husbands".

For a long time Banaz kept quiet about the abuse, but
eventually she told her parents and they spoke to Ali about
his behaviour. He agreed that he beat their daughter, but
explained that it was because she was disrespectful, and he
did force her to have sex, but only when she said no. According
to Banaz, her parents found this acceptable and sent her
back to try harder to be a better wife to her husband. She
recalled them "brainwashing" her into thinking that leaving a
husband would bring shame on them all. So much for
Mahmod's account of being aware of "minor" difficulties.

The abuse continued and, eventually, she grabbed a few
possessions and left their home in Coventry, returning to live
with her parents in Morden. At the time of her interview with
police, Banaz was already aware that her life was in danger.
She knew that divorce was frowned upon within her community. She told the female officer interviewing her that "men
are following me . . . If anything happens to me, it's them." At
the conclusion of the interview, Banaz turned to the interviewing officer and asked, "Now that I have given this statement, what can you do for me?"

There are two heartbreaking aspects to this statement
and they both relate to trust and betrayal. The first is the
awful life led by this young woman, who until a few weeks
before her marriage was still at school. Separated from her
family, living in another part of the country, wanting to please,

yet being physically and sexually abused. Not even knowing whether her husband's behaviour was normal. Asking for help from the people who should love and protect her and being told the fault was hers.

The second was the appalling betrayal by West Midlands Police, who were responsible for investigating the allegations and keeping Banaz safe. "What can you do for me?" she had asked. The truth is that a risk assessment should have been carried out and a comprehensive plan put in place to ensure her safety. Sadly, they did absolutely nothing. The investigating officer failed to trace the husband, who by now was living in Sheffield, and he did nothing about the men following her in the street. I will not repeat the language I used, but suffice to say I summoned the officer to London to explain his actions.

Next item in the file: on 4 December 2005, Banaz attended Wimbledon police station to report that her uncle Ari had threatened to kill her. She alleged that he had called her mother on the evening of the 2nd, on the landline at the family home. Banaz told the police some men who were following her had seen her kissing Rahmat. These men told her they had taken photographs of her and this had, in turn, been reported to Ari, who was the head of the family. Banaz's mother had told her that Ari had threatened to kill both Banaz and Rahmat for bringing shame on the community. Banaz said that her mother would not speak to the police and asked them not to approach Ari as that would make matters worse for her. She also described how leaving her husband was frowned upon in her community and described her father as having been brainwashed by Ari. She did not want the police to take any action, she said, she just wanted to make a record in case anything happened to her. Once again, she was allowed to leave a police station with no plan or measures put in place to keep her safe.

The following day a detective read the crime report and tried to put matters right. He called on Banaz at her family home. This is precisely what we now train officers *not* to do, for a woman cannot speak freely in front of her abusers, and exposing her for having contacted the police at all could make things worse. In fairness to the detective, that was what everyone did at the time – that officer knew no more about honour killings than I did in those days. He was just trying to do the right thing and look after Banaz.

Banaz kept him on the doorstep – he could tell she was anxious. Again, she said her mother would not speak to the police but this time she said her mother had put the phone on loudspeaker when Ari had called, so Banaz had heard Ari herself. Whether this was something she had omitted from her earlier statement or a way of putting the officer off speaking to her mother, we will never know.

On 12 December, Banaz hand-delivered her letter to Wimbledon police station. I read it through. She named five people who were going to be responsible for killing her. She provided their details, where they worked, even the colour of their cars. Once again, she was allowed to leave without any action being taken to keep her safe. The letter itself was not packaged or even brought to anyone's attention. Eventually it found its way to the same detective as before, who again tried to contact Banaz, this time by telephone. Banaz neither answered her phone nor responded to messages. Another precious opportunity had been missed.

Perhaps strangest of all, we had a crime report written by a female officer who had been called to a café in Wimbledon on New Year's Eve, where Banaz made the allegation that her father had tried to kill her. Banaz had clearly been drinking alcohol and she told the officer that her father had forced her to have some brandy at her grandmother's address nearby. She had injuries to her hands and she told the officer that in her efforts to escape from her father, she had smashed the window of an elderly neighbour.

The officer clearly didn't believe what she was being told. The tone of the report was contemptuous and pejorative. It contained phrases such as "Danaz [sic] then tried to tell me . . ." Her follow-up statement, when it arrived, was even more damning. By the time the officer wrote this statement, she was aware that Banaz was being treated as a high-risk missing person and that there was every chance she had been harmed. Yet, in her statement, the officer described Banaz as manipulative and melodramatic and implied she was making the whole story up to get Rahmat's attention.

This officer had not searched the crime scene itself to look for evidence. Neither had she reported Banaz's serious allegation to the CID. She did speak to Mahmod, but incredibly, instead of questioning him about Banaz's allegation, she told him she believed his daughter was lying in order to cover up the fact she had got herself drunk. "Mahmod sternly spoken to about making false allegations," read the report. Mahmod professed to be shocked to discover she had been drinking, and generously offered to pay for the damage to the window.

This crime report and statement were completely at odds with the accounts given by every other person who dealt with Banaz that night. None of these other witnesses knew Banaz or each other, they had no reason whatsoever to lie, yet everyone who encountered Banaz that night described her as being terrified.

Staff in the café said Banaz had been distraught. She had collapsed on the floor, bleeding from her hands and telling everyone her father had tried to kill her. She had also been terrified for Rahmat and gave the staff his number so that they could warn him. Banaz had then been taken to hospital to treat the injuries to her hands. Several nurses and paramedics said Banaz had to be coaxed out of the back of the ambulance and a security guard placed with her, so afraid was she that her father would find her. Later, one of the nurses who dealt with her burst into tears the second she was told Banaz was missing. She said she knew when Banaz discharged herself from hospital that something was going to happen to her.

The ambulance staff described the police officer as unsympathetic and uncaring. One stated that while Banaz was trying to tell the officer what had happened, the officer told her to shut up or she would arrest her for criminal damage. Reading that witness statement, my mind went back to the wording on the crime report. "Danaz then *tried* to tell me . . ."

What made this even more astonishing to me was that the officer had received specialist training: she was qualified as a sexual offences investigation trained officer (SOIT), somebody who supports and gathers evidence from victims of rape and serious sexual assault. She would know better than anybody that the strangest stories are the ones that often turn out to be true. Police have a sworn duty to protect life. That is our number one priority and the very first thing we learn in training. Even after knowing that a young girl was missing and her life could be at risk, the officer had chosen to speak against Banaz, rather than admit she might have made a mistake.

Luckily for us, we had one more piece of evidence to weigh up. The best account of all, as it turned out, came from Banaz herself.

Rahmat had taken a video of Banaz when she was in hospital on his mobile phone, and we now had that footage. In the office at Lewisham police station, the team sat mesmerised as we watched Banaz give her account. We so very rarely get to see our victim actually talking about what had happened to them. In the video, this beautiful young woman is lying on a hospital trolley. She looks very poorly and upset. She is speaking to Rahmat in Kurdish and even without the translation there is no mistaking her anguish. Her mouth is dry with dehydration and distress – you can see her licking her lips as she tries to speak. This is the account she gives.

Her father approached her while she was washing dishes at home. He told her to come with him as they were going to her grandmother's house to sort out her divorce from Ali. He said Ari and some others would be there. He then drove to her grandmother's house a different way to normal and when they arrived he told her to switch off her mobile phone and hand it over to him. As they got out of the car he handed her an empty suitcase and told her to carry it inside.

There was nobody at her grandmother's house. The curtains were pulled and it was very dark. Her father told Banaz to sit on the sofa and he gave her a bottle of brandy. She had never drunk alcohol before. He instructed her to drink it, saying it would help her to relax. He then started asking her questions about when she first met Rahmat. He kept returning to her, exhorting her to drink and asking her whether she felt sleepy.

When most of the bottle had been drunk, her father told her to look at the television. She was not to turn around and look at what he was doing. But something made her look over her shoulder and she caught her father creeping up on her, wearing disposable rubber gloves and trainers. Banaz knew in that second he was going to kill her.

She stood up, but her father pushed her back down onto the sofa and told her to keep drinking. He went back into another room to fetch something, at which point Banaz saw that the key was still in the back door. She made a dash for the door and by some miracle beat her father to it, escaping into the back garden. In an effort to get help, she plunged her hands through a window next door, cutting herself in the process. When help did not immediately arrive, she clambered over a wooden fence and staggered off up the road, collapsing on the floor of the Heart and Soul Café.

At one stage Rahmat asks her who did it and she replies "*Baba*", "Dad". There is something childlike in the way she says that name that is just heartbreaking.

I watched that video many, many times. I could see nothing in her behaviour that could even remotely be mistaken for manipulation or melodrama. There was nothing but distress and fear. How could the officer have interpreted it any other way? I do not understand it to this day. It was New Year's Eve, freezing cold. Banaz was wearing just a T-shirt and jeans. No shoes, no jumper, no coat, no bag, no mobile phone. She was bleeding from the hands and telling anybody who would listen, "My father just tried to kill me." What is there not to believe?

According to Rahmat's account, Banaz discharged herself from the hospital and went to stay with him for a couple of days. A nurse described her as having said, "If I stay here I am dead. If I go home I am dead." The family made contact with Banaz by telephone and begged her to come home. She and Rahmat agreed to meet Mahmod at McDonald's in nearby Tooting. According to Rahmat, Mahmod cried and kissed his hand. He said he should never have listened to his brother. He promised Banaz that she would not be harmed if she came home. The family preyed on Banaz's conscience, on her decency and on her love for them. The shame of her being absent from the home without their consent was affecting them all, they said.

Banaz returned home. What choice did she have? It was clear from our inquiries that she had no friends, no job – she was totally isolated and had no support network apart from Rahmat. And she loved her family. She wanted to believe that they were sorry, that she wouldn't be harmed. As in nearly all cases of domestic or child abuse, she just wanted the abusive behaviour to stop.

It was clear from her texts to Rahmat for the first few weeks in January 2006, that she had told her family that she would no longer see him, that she had given him up. It was also clear that neither of them in fact had the slightest intention of giving each other up. "There is no life for me without you," she told him. "Life wid out eachotha is hell and haram for us." Time was running out.

A few days later, the female officer called on Banaz at the family address. Not to enquire after her welfare, you understand. Instead she wanted Banaz to sign a form admitting she had smashed the window. Our compliant girl, of course, obliged.

The final opportunity to save Banaz came on 23 January in Hounslow when the men had tried to force Rahmat to get into the car with them. By now, Banaz had seen enough to know that both she and Rahmat were gravely at risk. When she went into Wimbledon police station, she was seen by a woman officer who was both supportive and sympathetic. Banaz told her that she was now willing to make a statement against her family. That officer, PC Alison Way, tried everything to get Banaz to come into a place of safety, but Banaz was adamant that she wanted to go home that night. She made an appointment to come back to the police station the following day to make the statement. She told the officer, "My mother is at home tonight. She will not let anything happen to me." She walked out of that police station and hasn't been seen since.

There were so many signs: the rape and physical assault by Ali Abass Homar; the threats to kill Banaz by Ari; another allegation of malicious communications; Banaz's letter naming the killers; and then, just days before Banaz went missing, the youngest daughter was being followed to and from school by the same group of men who had taken photos outside the café. While all this was going on, Banaz had trusted her family and she had trusted the system of the country she had come to call her own. Both had betrayed her trust.

This case was unlike any other: not only were we a homicide team investigating a case without a body, but we had oral and video statements about the possible murder from the victim herself, as well as her handwritten list of suspects. In fact, Banaz had given the police more than enough information to act. With a heavy heart I went downstairs to speak to my boss, Detective Superintendent Phil Adams, and tell him what I knew. Together, we decided to self-refer to the Independent Police Complaints Commission.

A "gold group" was immediately convened, chaired by Commander Simon Bray. The purpose of a gold group, which is chaired by a very senior officer, is to support the management of a critical incident with particular focus on the needs of the victim, their family and the community and any vulnerability to the reputation of the Metropolitan Police. I hadn't met Commander Bray before. I had so much going on already, the last thing I needed was to waste time at non-operational meetings and to have another senior officer giving me a grilling in front of a room full of people. I needn't have worried, though – Simon was charm personified and hugely supportive.

It didn't take long before people began to clamour for a public inquiry. I was aware that protestors had been making their presence felt outside various police stations. Placards bore Banaz's photograph, with the slogan "Justice for Banaz". It was a slogan I would see and hear a lot in the next few years.

OMERTA

I have worked with some fantastic people over the span of my 33-year career in the police. Some I remember for their determination, some for their wit and the sheer joy they bring to each day at work. I remember Detective Constable Sarah Raymond for her compassion. Sarah had come to us from the child protection team and was an expert in witness interviewing and care.

Sarah's role in the investigation was a crucial one, for she was the family liaison officer (FLO). Being an FLO is a very difficult and demanding job. You need to be extremely resilient, but at the same time caring and compassionate. It is one of the most vitally important roles of any murder investigation, not only because it provides that link between the senior investigating officer and the family, but because the evidence they gather from the family enables the team to "know" the victim. It helps us to understand their character, their habits, likes and dislikes. It humanises a person we might never have met in life and it helps us contextualise other information we receive about the murder.

Sarah duly set about interviewing the women of Banaz's family, all of whom were treated as significant witnesses. Her first impression was that none of them were telling the whole truth.

Sarah managed to interview all the sisters: Beza (28), Bekhal (22), Payman (18) and the youngest sister, who was still sixteen. According to Sarah's report, Beza was married to an extremely controlling husband. They had a young son who was the centre of the Mahmod family's world, no more than a toddler at that time. While Beza didn't live with her parents, she spent a great deal of time at their house.

Beza provided an account of the morning of 24 January, the date we suspected Banaz had gone missing. She stated that she, Beza, was upstairs at Morden Road. She fed the baby and then had a bath. When she came downstairs Banaz was not there and her bedding had been packed away. Sarah felt something was not right with Beza's statement, though she couldn't put her finger on any particular inconsistency.

Payman was also married and, like Beza, living away from the family home. She was the closest of all the sisters to Banaz, but could not provide any useful information about her disappearance. She was not thought to be a suspect.

On the first occasion that Sarah met Bekhal, she came away with the impression that Bekhal was frightened and wasn't revealing everything she knew. She was extremely guarded. Bekhal's own circumstances were very unusual for a woman from a Kurdish family as she was living outside the family home without their consent. In 2002, Mahmod had beaten her for being too westernised. She had made a physical abuse allegation, which resulted in her going into the care of Social Services at the age of sixteen. She was now living independently and was, therefore, unable to tell us anything about Banaz's disappearance.

Bekhal was initially reluctant to talk about her immediate family but did say she had left home because her father was too strict – again giving the lie to Mahmod's claim that he was a liberal parent. She was very fearful that her uncle Ari might have harmed Banaz. She described Ari as a "controlling arsehole" and said the men could do as they pleased but the girls had to adhere to a strict code of honour. There was competition, she said, between the girls in Mahmod's household and those in Ari's and their brother Johar's households as to who could be the most honourable. This resulted in them all telling tales on each other so that they wouldn't be under scrutiny themselves.

Bekhal provided Sarah with a story from her childhood that confirmed everything we feared. One day as she was leaving school, Bekhal was walking along with a friend, an Asian boy. Unbeknown to her at that time, she was being followed by one of Uncle Johar's sons, Azad. Bekhal sat down in the road between two parked cars so that she could have a cigarette without being seen. This was how they lived their lives, she explained, hiding from view, keeping a low profile, living a lie. Azad came up to the boy Bekhal was with and hit him in the face with his crash helmet. By the time Bekhal got home that day, the family had been told and she was in trouble. She described a meeting being held at which the whole family was present. Uncle Ari was presiding, while Bekhal and her mother sat on the floor in the middle of the room. Ari slapped the sole of his foot, a sign of disrespect, and told Bekhal that if she was his daughter she would be ashes by now. Mahmod might be afraid of the police, but he was not.

There was a theme emerging here – young women being followed by men in the family, family meetings with Ari presiding, women being held to account for their behaviour and threatened with death. Bekhal told Sarah that she had been in touch with Banaz during her unhappy marriage. Banaz had told her about the abuse she was suffering and had disclosed to her that Ali had threatened to bury her in the back garden. Bekhal had never met Rahmat and was unaware of his relationship with Banaz.

Now, Bekhal revealed to Sarah that she was also worried for her own safety. The fact that she was living outside the family home was unacceptable to the family. She had a black boyfriend, something that was hugely disapproved of, and she was pregnant. Any one of those three things would have been enough to put her at risk, she told us. She had been told by a well-wisher that she had been photographed by a man in Peckham, south east London. She also thought a Kurdish man had been looking at her on the bus.

At the team meeting after that first contact we tried to work out what was going on here. What on earth was this all about? First Banaz being followed, then the youngest sister, now Bekhal. Everything Bekhal was telling Sarah reinforced the view that multiple members of the Kurdish community were involved. Sarah's assessment of Bekhal was that she was afraid, withholding information and mistrustful of police. She felt there was more to come.

Reflecting on the accounts of the women, it was obvious that we simply didn't know enough about their culture to know what they might be omitting or even lying about, nor what their motives would be. Were they mourning the loss of a loved one but too afraid to assist police? Were they complicit? Did they know anything at all about what had happened or were they being kept in the dark by the men? In an investigation like this, every instinct in you as a human being wants nothing more than to put an arm around family members and comfort them. It was completely counter-intuitive to be querying their accounts and motives. It also went against everything I had experienced in my own life.

I desperately needed cultural advice, but it was such a small community I didn't know who to approach. Who could I trust not to go running back to the family with details of the investigation? I called up Brent Hyatt again. Ever since I had first contacted him about Banaz, he wouldn't leave me alone. He was like a little terrier, constantly ringing me when I was trying to deal with so many other people. But now I realised I needed him. Not only did he provide me with a couple of reliable community contacts, he also taught me a couple of important differences between honour-based violence and mainstream domestic violence.

Mainstream domestic violence is normally committed spontaneously, by one individual against another, behind closed doors, and is generally abhorrent to the community at large. Honour-based violence is planned and premeditated. It is committed using the maximum amount of brutality in order to send a message to the community. It is frequently committed by multiple perpetrators and the whole community will know about it and approve. "They won't be keeping quiet about it," Brent told me. "They will be proud of what they have done and they will be talking about it." I put that bit of advice away in my back pocket for later.

In early March, Bekhal told Sarah that she had started to receive threats to her life. By this time, she had begun to trust that Sarah only wanted to keep her safe. Bekhal stated that she had received a telephone call from a Kurdish man, telling her that she was going to be the "next" girl to be killed – that she would get the same as Banaz. (Did that mean that Banaz was already dead?) The man also told her she was being followed. This resonated with the information she had given earlier on about being watched on the bus and photographed in the street.

Four or five weeks into the investigation, the team were now becoming much more aware of the realities of honour-based violence and took this new information very seriously. As Sarah started to explore with Bekhal who that threat might have come from, Bekhal began for the first time to open up about her immediate family.

When Bekhal was a teenager, Mahmod beat her for wanting to wear make-up, for wanting to wear western clothing. He beat her for plucking her eyebrows. On one occasion, he had been lying in wait for her as she walked home from school through a nearby park. He caught her with her head uncovered and he beat her for that. While Bekhal was in care, Mahmod had tried everything within his power to get her to come home, but Bekhal had been too fearful. It wasn't out of love for his daughter that Mahmod had wanted her to come home, but because her defiance made Mahmod look weak. Indeed, in 2003 Mahmod himself had reported to the police that he was getting abuse from the Kurdish community. Because Bekhal was in care, he was being perceived as unable to control his daughters – the family were being ostracised. Mahmod then slipped Bekhal a cassette tape under the nose of a social worker. The recording was in Kurdish. In it, Mahmod threatened Bekhal that if she did not come home he would murder her mother and her sisters. He would burn them alive and she would never see any of them again. Her mother could be heard weeping and telling Bekhal that her father meant what he said. Bekhal also told Sarah that in 2002, her brother, Bahman, had tried to kill her.

Sarah had been absolutely meticulous not to repeat what she was told by one family member to another. That meant Bekhal knew nothing at all about what had happened to Banaz on New Year's Eve. The account she now provided to Sarah about the attempt on her own life bore horrifying similarities.

Bahman called her to arrange a meeting, telling her that he had found a cleaning job for her. Bekhal was short of money and agreed to meet him in a park near Wimbledon police station. The spot where they met was quiet and not overlooked. Bahman handed her a suitcase and told her to carry it. As he did so, Bekhal noticed her brother was wearing "doctors' gloves" underneath motorcycle gauntlets. He ordered her to walk along a narrow path in front of him and told her not to turn around and look at him. She did as her brother asked. Bahman smashed her over the head with a dumbbell, leaving her barely conscious. She described herself holding onto his legs and begging him, "Please don't do this. I will do anything. Just tell Father you killed me and let me go." The pair of them, her and Bahman, sat on a park bench together, both of them crying, Bahman sobbed like a baby, saying, "Sorry, Bekhal, Dad said I had to kill you. You are bringing shame on the family."

We discovered that Bekhal had reported that assault to the police, too. We traced the original crime report, her statement and the hospital records. She had received seven stitches to a head wound. The police investigation was so scant it was disgusting. They hadn't even had her injury

photographed. She had been told to go away and find out if
the area was covered by CCTV. If it wasn't, it was basically
her word against Bahman's. That and the seven stitches in
her head.

Bekhal also told Sarah about having been subjected to
female genital mutilation (FGM) as a child. She had been
cut by her grandmother. She described being forcibly held
down by a number of female relatives while her grandmother
cut her. Bekhal had struggled so violently that her grandmother had cut her very deeply and she was still suffering the
effects to that day. It was very common for girls to be cut in
this way, Bekhal told us. FGM was something I did know all
about, coming from a background in Child Protection. It was
another means of controlling women's sexuality and reinforc-
ing a patriarchal society.

Intelligence suggested that the man who had called
Bekhal to warn her that "she would be next" was a close
member of the family. He was also thought to be a friend of
her brother's and was said to work with Dana Amin, the
young man who had been so keen to show Richard
Vandenburgh the boot of his Lexus. The caller wanted to
meet Bekhal, but she wisely refused, despite being asked
again and again. Intelligence also told us that the caller had
offered £1,000 to some unidentified Kurdish men to kill
Bekhal, and that he had been given a severe beating by a
different group of Kurdish men who mistakenly believed that
he was withholding where Bekhal lived.

I was petrified that something would happen to her. We
discussed the Witness Protection Scheme, but Bekhal was
reluctant to give up everything and everyone she knew. In fairness, she was never going to be a witness for us as she couldn't
say what had happened to her sister. Instead we put in a

number of measures to try to keep her safe. We took her DNA, fingerprints and photograph in case she went missing. We gave her panic alarms, built safe rooms, put cameras on her home. You name it, we did it. We provided her with a mobile phone and arranged for her to text Sarah with a new word every day, just so we would know she was still alive. How many times Bekhal forgot to text Sarah I can't tell you, but it was generally on a Sunday evening as I was serving the dinner that I would get a call from Sarah: "Sorry to disturb you, Guvnor, but Bekhal hasn't called in." We would drop everything and track her down, and thankfully she was always OK.

We moved that poor young woman from address to address. In April, the risk escalated further still when Bekhal reported that she was getting calls from her sister Payman's husband, Sala Abdullah, demanding a meeting. Meanwhile, the rest of the team were still searching for Banaz.

In the initial search and arrest phase, we had not managed to arrest Mohammed Hama. He was one of the men who had tried to abduct Rahmat on 22 January and was also on Banaz's list of suspects. He was not at his address in Uffington Road, West Norwood, but his hired Ford Focus was. Present in the flat was a man who claimed to be the lawful occupier. He gave his name as Alan Hama, although he denied emphatically that he was related to Mohammed. He told officers that Mohammed Hama didn't live there, he just stayed from time to time. Judging from the amount of possessions belonging to Mohammed at the address, this was clearly untrue. A search of the flat revealed a photograph of Mohammed, together with Mohammed Ali and Omar Hussain, posing by a vehicle. Just three regular guys, enjoying a day out together.

Finding the vehicle was useful to us as it corroborated Rahmat's account of the attempted kidnap on 22 January and provided us with forensic opportunities. At the very least we hoped it would provide forensic evidence to link Mohammed Hama, Omar and Mohammed Ali to the vehicle, and to iden-tify the fourth man in the vehicle and any other associates who may provide other lines of enquiry. It might also prove whether Banaz had ever been in the car. We also seized three mobile phones and two SIM cards. We noted that Alan himself had a driving licence application signed by Ari Mahmod. We left a message with Alan: tell Mohammed Hama to hand himself in; we need to speak to him.

Much to our surprise, Hama did just that. Supremely confident and apparently well prepared, he walked into Lewisham police station on 2 February 2006 and was duly arrested.

Unlike the other suspects we had interviewed, Hama spoke. He agreed that he had been present at the meeting at Ari Mahmod's house on 2 December. Just like Ari, he claimed that the meeting was to welcome Ari's new son-in-law. There was a grain of truth in that – Ari had collected his son-in-law from the airport that very day. But all the best lies have a grain of truth. When asked about Banaz and Rahmat, Hama said that it had been mentioned only in passing that they were in a relationship. The men had commented how happy they were for them both. It was exactly the same story as Ari had originally given, almost to the letter, and sounded horri-bly rehearsed.

We asked him about the incident at Hounslow. Hama agreed that he had been in the car with Mohammed Ali and Omar Hussain. In relation to the fourth man he became very vague – he didn't know him, didn't know whose friend he was, didn't even know his name. He was just the driver, you understand. Hama denied emphatically making any threats.

No, he said, it was all very friendly. He couldn't imagine why Rahmat would make up such a wicked lie – Rahmat had been a friend of all of them for years. He did say that Omar had a slight problem with Rahmat, who had lied about his relationship with Banaz. Rahmat had promised Omar he had given Banaz up and Omar had found out this wasn't true. Omar just wanted to discuss this with Rahmat, but there were definitely no threats. When asked, he could not explain why Rahmat's relationship with Banaz was Omar's business.

On 3 February, no sooner had we got Hama in custody than Rahmat got in touch to say he had received a phone call from a Kurdish man, saying that Banaz was still alive. "I swear on the Holy Qur'an, brother," the man had said, "she is alive." The caller promised to find out where she was and wanted Rahmat to meet him. Poor Rahmat was absolutely beside himself, not knowing what to believe. He wanted to believe it was true, of course, but we had doubts. We counselled him to be cautious, because it could be a trap to lure him into a meeting and kill him. He knew we were right but it was very painful for him, nevertheless.

Identifying the young man who was now calling Rahmat was not an easy matter. We already had nine suspects in custody at that particular time, and were more than fully employed with interviews and ongoing surveillance operations against others. Another manhunt we did not need – but could it lead us to Banaz?

Rahmat thought he knew the caller's first name but we had no address and he was using a pre-pay phone. This was one of the biggest challenges we faced in the inquiry – identifying who was who and working out who was related. The Kurdish naming system is usually a given name, followed by the father's name, followed by the grandfather's name. That should be simple enough, but it doesn't always work out that way. Many of these men had entered the country as illegal immigrants using false documents. Others swapped the order of their names around or adopted English given names. Some used different names with different people. Some had nicknames. (Thus, for example, Mohammed Hama also went by the names Mohammed Marif or Marefa and was also known as Soora, meaning "red" or "ginger".) Additionally, men who had completed the Haj pilgrimage might take the name Haji (so Mohammed Ali was also referred to as Haji Ali or Saleh Ali). Throw into the mix the Arabic script, which does not transliterate exactly into English, and one name may be spelled in several different ways. Seventeen ways if your name is Mohammed.

With Rahmat's caller, we suspected he might be related to one of the people we had in custody, but didn't know for sure. Suppose he had Banaz? Using Rahmat as what is termed a "tasked witness", we tried to get this young man to come into a police station or meet us, but he was having none of it. Should we show Rahmat a photo of a potential suspect and then blow any later identification? Should we release the person we suspected was related to the caller and hope he took us to the caller's address or an address where Banaz was? Was it all just a ruse to stall for time? Did they want to kill Rahmat?

That day I found out that one of my team, John Smith, had been taken into hospital with peritonitis. We had been new recruits together back in the eighties. He hadn't wanted to say anything because he knew the job needed doing and didn't want to let me down. I had a damn good cry at that moment. What sort of guvnor was I? I wasn't looking after my people. I didn't even know he was ill. When did I last speak to him? Looking around me, I began to see that I was burning people out. Craigy told me that Claire Elliott in the intel team was also feeling unwell. She looked worn out, sitting in a puffer jacket next to a portable radiator. She refused to go home that day, but it turned out that she had pneumonia.

As if that wasn't bad enough, I then took a call from a young woman I had never met to say that my oldest son, away at university, had been admitted to hospital. He had developed a quinsy in his throat and needed an operation. I promised myself I would call him the next day before he went under the general anaesthetic. The next day, however, was just as frantic as the one before. I looked up at the clock and realised, with horror, that I had missed my opportunity to speak to my son. Lousy guvnor, lousy mother. More tears but, to be honest, I didn't have the time for self-pity.

I spent days trying to track down this mystery caller, praying to God we were going to find Banaz alive. The Police and Criminal Evidence Act 1984 dictates how long suspects can be held in custody and I was running out of time with Mohammed Hama. It is the duty of police officers to investigate all of the facts, not just those that support their hypothesis. Thus, I had to exhaust all reasonable lines of inquiry to establish whether Banaz was still alive, even though I suspected the caller was being untruthful. While half of the team were out searching for the caller, using every means at their disposal, my custody clock was ticking away. It was becoming increasingly obvious that the young man calling Rahmat had simply been prevaricating, wasting time in the hope that Hama would be released. If the girl wasn't dead, Hama couldn't be charged with murder, right?

Wrong. Rahmat had now positively identified Mohammed Hama as the man who had made threats to kill him and

Banaz on 22 January 2006. I made a decision that if we hadn't found the caller or Banaz by midnight, I was going to ask the Crown Prosecution Service (CPS) for permission to charge Hama with conspiracy to murder.

I had been liaising with the CPS from the outset of the investigation. The senior Crown prosecutor was a woman called Damaris Lakin, who I knew from previous murder investigations. She was highly intelligent and fiercely independent, a plain speaker and not someone to suffer fools gladly; the evidence is either there or it isn't. Damaris had offered to keep this horribly complex case herself rather than have me try to explain it to an out-of-hours lawyer over the phone. I would have struggled to brief anyone new in the time available.

True to her word, Damaris answered the phone at midnight. Her advice was that the evidence was just sufficient to charge Hama, but the charge should be one of murder, not conspiracy. Hama had been positively identified as threatening to kill Banaz by Rahmat, whose evidence was corroborated in many other areas. The texts showed their relationship was disapproved of, contrary to Hama's claims. The threats, coupled with Banaz's disappearance two days later, was sufficient to charge him with her murder.

It was a brave decision to make. Once you have charged someone with an offence you have a time limit to bring the case before the court for trial. I couldn't even prove that Banaz was dead, much less that Hama had killed her.

The alternative was to bail him in the same way we had with Mahmod, Ari and the others, but Omar Hussain had already fled the country and in all probability Mohammed Ali had as well. I feared that if we bailed Mohammed Hama we would never see him again. Unlike Ari and Mahmod, he had no home or family here and thus, no incentive to remain.

The following morning Detective Superintendent Phil Adams told me that the commander, Dave Johnston, was not altogether in agreement with my course of action. He had apparently asked whether "that wee lassie knows what she's doing".

At first, this wee lassie was a bit put out and I wondered whether he would have asked a male SIO the same question. Of course he was right to ask, it was his job to ask. I was only "acting up" in the rank, it was my first job as SIO and it was a case that would challenge even the most experienced. I didn't relish the comment, though. Of course I didn't know what I was doing. I hadn't dealt with anything like this in my life. Neither had anyone else as far as I knew. I was just doing the best I could. I was trained and experienced; everything was thought through and well reasoned. I could only hope I had made the right decision.

One benefit of keeping Mohammed Hama in custody was that it allowed us to covertly record his conversations. Brent Hyatt had reckoned that the suspects would be talking, and even boasting about what they had done. Time would tell.

OUR GIRL

Merton, February 2006

There are some moments of the investigation that I remember with absolute clarity and the phone call from Rick Murphy was one of them.

I had gone home for the night to get some shut-eye. It was one of the first opportunities I'd had for a good night's sleep since the investigation began. My head hit the pillow and I was out like a light. I must have been asleep for about half an hour or so when the mobile went. It was Rick. He was whispering down the phone. He was also in bed, trying not wake his missus. "Just had a call from Ms Ali. Sounds like those fuckers have killed her and put her in a suitcase."

I was instantly wide awake. Ms Ali was our interpreter and we had tasked her with translating the recordings of Mohammed Hama's conversations. My heart sank. It confirmed our worst fears.

"The tapes are difficult to hear," he went on, "but they are saying she is in a suitcase, under some stones, in the water."

My mind was racing. What could it mean? I thought of Lesley Whittle, the poor young woman who was abducted and murdered in 1975 by Donald Neilson. Her body had been found hanging in a ventilation shaft. Was Banaz in a drain somewhere? We started kicking suggestions back and forth between us, each lying in our respective beds, next to our sleeping partners, whispering down the phone at each other.

"Ms Ali thinks they mean millstones, like possibly she is under a water mill."

Now Morden was as far removed in my mind from the bucolic idyll watermill scene as could be imagined and I said so. "That's a lot of fucking use, innit? There's not exactly a lot of those in Morden."

"That's just it. I've just googled it, there are five within a couple of miles of her house. They're right on the River Wandle and the river was used for the breweries."

I won't repeat the expletives that followed but suffice to say I was out of bed in a flash, putting in place plans for the next day.

The following day was a Saturday and it was properly bitter. It was that type of cold that permeates every layer of clothing, with that raw wind that makes eyes and noses stream. The team assembled in the park opposite Banaz's house, a National Trust property of some 120 acres. The River Wandle passes within yards of Banaz's house, goes under her road and emerges into the park. In addition to the river itself, the park features a couple of large lakes and an area of marshland. It would be the perfect place to dispose of a body.

We were met by a specialist underwater search team and a specialist search advisor. There is a scientific process to determining the order of search locations when looking for homicide victims, based on a wide body of research. It was a huge area and we needed to prioritise where to start. To complicate matters further, a local woman had called police to say that she had been walking her dog in the marsh area when the dog had become excited about something and disappeared into the marshes. When it returned, its muzzle had been covered in blood.

The park manager informed us that those marshes could be drained, so we duly arranged for that to be done, which took several hours. In the meantime, we cracked on with searching the river. Once the marshes were drained, we arranged for a specialist dog unit to search the area. I remember us taking the mickey out of the handler because the dog didn't want to get his feet wet, but you couldn't blame him. It was freezing. The dog went in eventually, but he didn't find anything.

That icy water caused us further problems. The underwater search team could only go in the water for three quarters of an hour at a time, due to health and safety concerns, and only twice a day. We weren't going to make very good progress at that rate. As the daylight faded, the team reconvened in a nearby pub to warm up and debrief.

The underwater team were willing to come out again the following day – of course they were on "double bubble", as we call overtime rates – but we just weren't getting the area covered quickly enough. Although murder teams have a larger budget than most, we are still accountable for every penny we spend.

DC Nick Stocking, ever reliable, hit on a good solution. He had recently arranged a demonstration of a private specialist search team for a team training day and had their details. This team consisted of ex-servicemen who specialised in searching difficult areas. They were a tough bunch and, shall we say, not as constrained by health and safety regulations as the public sector. We gave them a call. Not only would they come out tomorrow, but they would provide sonar towing equipment and would guarantee to cover the whole area in two days. Result!

On the drive home we reflected on the search. We just couldn't get over the fact that not one person from Banaz's family had asked us how it was going or whether there was any news. Most of us were parents ourselves and could not comprehend their indifference. Anyone who has had a teenager late home from an evening out will know that gut-wrenching worry. I can only imagine what it must be like to have a child go missing for any length of time – I would be beside myself.

There were dozens of us in the park that day with marked police vehicles and frogmen. We had drawn the curiosity of half the neighbourhood, who had gathered to watch us work. Not the Mahmods, though. Not one of them had come out of their house to speak to us. They showed no interest at all.

Everybody deserves to be loved. To have not a single soul worry about you when you are missing is such a sad concept. Right there and then in the car, Rick and I decided that if her own parents didn't love her, then we would become her surrogate parents – we would love her. She was "our girl". She was part of the Team 16 family.

Over the next few days we searched miles of the River Wandle. The specialist search team were true to their word and covered huge areas of water. I have one image that will always stay with me. We were searching an area of the river close to Merton Abbey Mills, which is a pretty location by south London standards. Five men in frogmen's suits were wading line abreast through chest-deep icy water, making their way towards the mills. Suddenly a van pulled up outside the mills and half a dozen men got out and started putting on wetsuits. Even more confusing was the fact that someone else was setting up a camera on a tripod. What the hell was going on? Had someone tipped off a news team?

Even at a distance I could see the confusion and annoyance of both those in the water and those in the van. There was lots of exaggerated gesticulating and shrugging and squaring of shoulders occurring on both sides. I sent someone over to the van to find out what was going on. It transpired that the crew in the van were actors. They were there to film an episode for *The Bill*, which involved an underwater search. We politely asked them to come back another day.

Meanwhile, the covert recordings of Mohammed Hama were beginning to bear more fruit. We had the tapes of a conversation with Alan Hama cleaned up and translated by Ms Ali and a colleague. True to Brent's advice, Mohammed was boasting about what he had done, even laughing about it. The translation, when we read it, was horrific.

"They were slapping her, fucking her, I fucked her anally. I couldn't get it in her mouth, I stuck it in her arse. Mohammed [Ali] made the cord like a hook and I said, 'Put it around quickly.' When she heard that, she was terrified, she was vomiting. I was stamping on her head. I had my foot on her back and I was pulling, pulling so hard. I wound the cord around her neck so tightly it was cutting into her flesh. It took the bitch more than half an hour for the soul to leave the body."

Reading that was like being sucker punched. Although we knew the chances of her being alive were slim, we had refused to give up hope. The conversations didn't specifically refer to Banaz by name but it was almost certainly her they were talking about. It was hard to imagine the terror she must have faced. She had been lying on a mattress in the living room, wearing only her knickers, just about to get up and go to the police station to make her statement. Can you imagine the horror of lying in bed and having three men burst into your room? She must have known at that point that she was going to be killed. And then being raped and then slowly strangled, gasping for air for half an hour, praying for salvation that didn't come?

There was another bombshell in the translation: Hama talked about Beza, the eldest daughter. "Beza was there. Ari lied to us, the bastard. He said the house would be empty, but Beza was there." That was a turn-up as far as the team were concerned. Beza had told us that she was upstairs feeding the baby and taking a bath. She had claimed that she hadn't heard or seen a thing, but here was one of the murderers saying Beza was in the house when the murder was taking place. The house was tiny – it's not as if you could miss each other in there. We couldn't say at that point that Banaz had been murdered at her home address, but she had, at least, been abducted from there.

This raised a number of questions about Beza. How had the murderers gained entry to the house? Had she let them in? The murderers weren't expecting her to be there, so it seemed more likely that Ari had given them a key. In that case, Beza would probably have been terrified when those men entered her parents' home unexpectedly, intent on killing her sister. Beza had told us that when she came downstairs, all of Banaz's bedding had been neatly folded and put away. That seemed highly unlikely, unless our three murderers were particularly

tidy by nature. Had Beza packed away that bedding? Did her
parents put the bedding away when they returned? We couldn't
go back and challenge her because we didn't want anyone to
know we were recording Hama's conversations.

There was more in that conversation. Hama commented
that they had made a mistake in leaving her passport at the
address. If they had taken it, the family could have pretended
she had run away. He talked about stamping on her head and
putting the body in a suitcase and described Ari dragging it
along a road. "The road was crowded and a police car came
by. Cars were passing by and we were dragging the bag. The
handle broke off. Man, I swear, I was standing there, I almost
ran away."

"Who was dragging it?" asked Alan Hama.

"Mr Ari. We were around him on each side, as God is my
witness. Her hair was sticking out and her elbow."

Mohammed Hama said he was afraid his fingerprints and
DNA would be discovered. They talked about putting the
suitcase in a car and driving it somewhere – but we had no
idea where that somewhere was. We did, however, know that
the car was driven by someone called Dana. Could this be
our cocky Lexus driver?

Then he talked about the fact that they had buried the
suitcase in a back garden somewhere. Mohammed said that
"she started to smell, even in one night". So she had been
buried on the day following her murder.

"I buried it so deep they will only find it if there is an
informant. I took it under the house." According to
Mohammed Hama, Mohammed Ali had dropped the suitcase clumsily into the hole, fracturing what sounded like an
elbow on a water pipe. "Omar", he said, "was terrified. He
was not a man."

The house, wherever it was, belonged to friends of Omar Hussain. Once the pipe had started leaking, the two Mohammeds had called a Kurdish plumber to try to fix it, but to no avail. The occupants of the house had now fled. Mohammed Hama told Alan to go and see "Pakiza's man" and "bring me the news". Pakiza was Ari's wife. Hama talked about fleeing the country if he got out on bail.

Appalled as we were at learning of that awful murder, we felt we were at last beginning to see the true shape of events. If the knot wasn't exactly undone, I had, at least, found the end of the string: we had Omar and the two Mohammeds at Mahmod's house murdering or abducting Banaz with Beza upstairs. We had Ari making the arrangements and Dana driving the body somewhere to be buried. The difficulty was that we had absolutely none of this evidentially. We had been told in no uncertain terms by the people who deal with prison intelligence that we could never, under any circumstances, use the taped conversations in evidence.

We needed to find a way of proving what we knew and proving it quickly. While we had enough evidence to charge Mohammed Hama, we didn't have enough to convict him, and what we had might not even survive an application to dismiss the case, or even a bail hearing. It was no longer a race against time to find Banaz alive – it was a race to find her body before Hama was released from prison.

We had completed all of the fast-time actions and were now bedding in for the long haul. Most of us were at least getting home at night some of the time. The majority of murders are solved within the first few weeks and it is far easier to maintain momentum and morale when things are happening quickly and people can see results. It requires a different sort of leadership altogether when an inquiry becomes a gritty war of attrition.

I had now gone from a position of struggling to keep the investigation from running away to struggling to keep it moving, ensuring no stone was left unturned and nobody got careless. A "sticker", as these cases are known, requires determination, thoroughness, tenacity and a systematic approach. I held regular formal meetings, but the informal ones were just as, if not more, effective. Craigy always says some of our best decisions were made over a beer and I don't disagree. Apart from anything else, it was important to be able to let off steam together. Cops are never short of a story or two to tell, usually at each other's expense.

Meanwhile, more and more recordings were being translated of conversations Hama was having with several Kurdish men. We were astounded at the sheer number of men who simply couldn't wait to get involved. They wanted to show their support and, in so doing, enhance their own reputation. At one point, Hama commented, "I have done justice." That absolutely summed up the mindset.

Two of the men he spoke to were friends of Rahmat's, Darbaz and Pshtwan. They had been there on 22 January when Hama and the others had tried to abduct Rahmat – in fact, Darbaz had stepped in to defend Rahmat. Hama instructed the two friends to lie to the police: tell them we sat and discussed football, and that was it – there were no threats.

Sure enough, when it came to interviewing those two friends of Rahmat's, they both trotted out the same story. All the men had sat and drank tea together, they said. They talked about Manchester United. No threats were made to Rahmat.

So now our case was getting even weaker. We had been relying on Rahmat positively identifying Hama as making threats
to kill Banaz and him. Now, Rahmat's two best friends were
saying he was lying. We knew why they were saying it, but,
again, we couldn't challenge their accounts without revealing
that we were recording the conversations. We knew what they
had done – we just couldn't prove it.

THE TIMELINE

Using information gleaned from cars, laptops and phones, Keilly put together a minute-by-minute timeline of events. By painstakingly reconstructing the timeline using everything we had seized, we got a potential lead about where the body might be.

One of the exhibits from Ari's house was the computer belonging to his daughter, Ala. The family were giving us all kinds of hell about homework and other rubbish, trying to get the computer back. We submitted it for analysis but were not expecting the result we got. There, on the hard drive, miraculously saved somehow, was an MSN conversation between Ala and a cousin. It was timestamped the evening of 2 December, the time when Ari had invited the men of the family for a meeting at his home. The story we had been fed by Mohammed Hama and Ari was that this was purely to welcome the new son-in-law and the only mention of Banaz was to say how happy they were to hear of her new relationship. The MSN conversation blew that story out of the water completely.

Ala was upstairs, listening to the men's conversation and giving a contemporaneous blow-by-blow account to her cousin, daughter of Ari and Mahmod's brother Johar. Ala was disgusted at what she was hearing. Having an affair is *haram* (forbidden), she wrote, and Banaz would go to hell, "but the girl doesn't deserve to die for it". Banaz had made all of the other girls look bad. At one stage, she wrote of her father and the other Kurdish men: "Motherfucking Kurds. This is some-one's life. Who cares what these fucking immigrant butchers think. None of them are innocent."

Then she told her cousin that she had already warned her mother. "I told her that if I find out anyone is going to kill her I will go to the police myself." Her cousin immediately coun-selled her to take care. "Be careful, Ala. Don't say stuff like that to them or they will kill you next." She stated her mother had been furious and said, "You would go to the police and let your family down?" It was a real-time, genuine snapshot of what was happening at Ari Mahmod's house that night. In an inquiry in which we were being provided with so much false information, it was gold dust.

Discreetly, we approached Ala, ensuring we did not put her in any danger by making an open approach. Ari would be livid if he knew Ala had sent that message. Ala shrugged the conver-sation off as nothing more than a light-hearted joke, but it was clearly more than that. But no matter how good it was, I couldn't use it as evidence for fear of getting those girls killed.

On a much more positive front, we learned that the hired Ford Focus used by Mohammed Hama, Mohammed Ali and Omar Hussain had, unbeknown to the murderers, had a tracker fitted. We examined the data for 22 January and noted that it showed the vehicle had stopped for barely a couple of minutes outside the friends' house in Hounslow.

This was enough to contradict the accounts given by Darbaz and Pshtwan. We duly arrested them for perverting the course of justice. Both admitted lying and blamed Omar, stating that he had threatened them. Both were charged and remanded into custody. It wasn't helping to convict Mohammed Hama, but it was, at least, limiting the damage those two could do.

Keilly was working like a Trojan to make sense of all the communications data from the suspects' mobile telephones. The initial strategy had been to identify a series of events, such as the meeting at Ari's house or the Hounslow incident, and try to prove or negate the allegations around them. The communications data showed the following:

2 December 2005 was the day on which Ari held that meeting at his house and on which Banaz had alleged that he rang her mother to tell her that Banaz and Rahmat would be killed.

17:34 Ari Mahmod's mobile calls the landline at Banaz's home address for 13 minutes. We had already established that Mahmod was not at home at that time and Behya, Banaz's mother, had agreed that Ari called her about Banaz that evening, even if she couldn't remember whether or not he threatened to kill her daughter. The evidence of this call corroborated Banaz's account.

17:47 Immediately after that call, Banaz sends Rahmat a text: "I need to speak to you urgently."

17:53 Banaz sends another text: "Go outside, I need to talk to you."

18:24 She texts after they finish speaking on the phone: "Don't call Ari or those idiots."

20:57 Banaz texts Rahmat again, giving the names of the people who were going to kill her.

The MSN conversation between Ala and her cousin occurs between 22:54 and 23:59.

22:54 The cousin asks Ala, "Is my Dad [Johar] there yet."

23:13 Ala replies, "Everyone's arriving."

23:41 Ari calls Mahmod's landline. Mahmod is at home when this call takes place.

23:54 Ari calls Mahmod's landline again.

00:07 Banaz texts Rahmat: "Uncle Ari called my Mum to discuss me and you. My Dad said he had guests and Ari said we can talk in the car. My Mum won't tell me anything. I will find out. Take extra care – I love you."

Something had happened that night that made it urgent for Banaz to text Rahmat at just gone midnight and discuss what Ari had said on the phone, warning him to take care. The conversation between Ala and her cousin makes it clear that a discussion had taken place about killing Banaz.

We were not certain where or when the murder had taken place, but we favoured the morning of 24 January at her home address since Banaz had not texted Rahmat that morning. Keilly's analysis showed the following:

- On 21 January Ari Mahmod calls Omar Hussain four times. This is highly unusual. In fact, the only other time we could see any communication between them was 2 December, the day of the meeting. One of those calls to Omar was made from the home address of Mohammed Ali.

- The following day, Omar's phone leaves his home address in Birmingham and comes to London. Mohammed Hama's vehicle and phone go to join Omar in Brixton and they travel together to Hounslow. Rahmat, Pshtwan and Darbaz all now agree that threats were made to kill Rahmat and Banaz outside the address in Hounslow. On the return journey, Ari calls Omar, presumably to ask whether he has accomplished the task of abducting Rahmat. There are also several calls from Rahmat to Omar, and Rahmat to Mahmod, and Rahmat to Ari, corroborating Rahmat's account.
- The phones and tracker show that Omar and Hama, having failed in their task, spend the night of the 22nd at Hama's address in Uffington Road, SE27.
- On 23 January, the day Banaz and Rahmat make their final reports to their respective police stations, Ari rings Omar at 11:52. Omar and Hama then go to Ari's building site in Wandsworth Road, Mohammed Ali's address in Brixton, then to Hama's address, then to Ari Mahmod's home address at Sandy Lane, Mitcham. While this is happening, Banaz sends Rahmat the text telling him to be careful, and that she loves him.
- Banaz's last text message to Rahmat says that she has been in touch with Steve, the West Midlands Police officer who was investigating her rape allegation. According to Banaz, Steve has told her to talk to the local police. (When I subsequently asked the officer about this call, he claimed not to be able to remember speaking to her, although the call was clearly in her billing data.) Later that day she makes

her last ever call to Rahmat, telling him that she is going back to the police station the following day to make a statement. They never speak again.

- That night Omar and Hama go once more to Mohammed Ali's Brixton address before spending the night at Mohammed Hama's place in West Norwood.

- On the morning of the 24th, Mahmod and Behya's accounts state they left 225 Morden Road at 08:30 to take their youngest daughter to school. Ari's mobile phone is used shortly afterwards in the vicinity of Banaz's home address. Keilly also found CCTV footage of his green Vitara vehicle being driven towards Banaz's house.

- At 08:55 and 09:40, Ari is in contact with Mohammed Ali and Omar, both of whom are also in the vicinity of Banaz's home address. By late morning Ari goes to the building site at Wandsworth Road, then to Mohammed Ali's address, then to Hama's address.

- Hama does not use his mobile that morning and the Ford Focus remains stationary outside his house. But the fact that Omar spent the night there and was subsequently cell-sited near Banaz's home address implies that somebody came to collect him.

- That afternoon, Omar Hussain's mobile shows him travelling back up to Birmingham.

- At 13:30, the Focus starts up and travels almost to Ari's house at Sandy Lane, Mitcham. The vehicle tracker is far, far more accurate than mobile phone location data and can place the vehicle within a few yards. The vehicle suddenly changes course just before it reaches Sandy Lane and goes instead to Wandsworth Road. It parks up just around the corner and stays there until the evening of the 25th.

- Later, on the afternoon of the 24th, the mobile phones belonging to Mohammed Ali and Mohammed Hama make their way up the motorway to Birmingham. They are clearly together in a vehicle, but not the Focus.

Before this, we had just a hypothesis about what had happened – now, we were beginning to fill in the blanks. For the few days leading up to Banaz's disappearance, all of our suspects were in contact with each other far more than would usually be the case. Omar Hussain came down from Birmingham, failed to abduct Rahmat and threatened to kill Banaz and Rahmat. The suspects spent the day of the 23rd together and then there was a period the following morning when they were all in contact with each other in the vicinity of Banaz's address (except for Hama, who didn't use either his phone or his car).

We knew that Banaz had been seen by her parents on the morning of the 24th, but she had failed to contact Rahmat as usual. We also knew from the recordings that she had either been abducted or killed while her sister Beza was in the house, which was on the 24th. Nothing in the recordings suggested she had been taken from the house alive. The home address was a semi-detached house on a busy main road and Banaz was in a state of undress. A live abduction would have been very hard to achieve. It did seem, therefore, that she had been murdered at her home. So, we thought we had the when and where of the murder, but where on earth was the body?

Having dragged the waterways and having already searched all of the known addresses, some several times, we thought back to the night of the 24th when Ari was having a bonfire at Wandsworth Road. We had already searched the remains of the fire and found nothing, but the property was under renovation. One of the lads remembered that a new marble floor had recently been fitted. We went back and smashed the new floor to pieces and looked underneath – nothing. We re-examined Mahmod's garden and the allotment. Nothing.

"She is in a suitcase, under some stones, in the water." What on earth did it mean? Ms Ali, the interpreter, had thought it meant a millstone. But there was an address associated with Omar Hussain at Windmill Close, in Birmingham. There was a huge mural of a windmill on the side of the house. Birmingham, of course, has miles of canals, so where did we start looking? Suddenly we were seeing windmills and watermills everywhere. With the arrival of the phone and tracker data, we could sense a breakthrough. Mohammed Ali and Mohammed Hama had gone to Birmingham in the late afternoon of the 24th and stayed there throughout the next day. In his taped conversation, Hama had commented that the body had started to smell after just one night, so there was a possibility, just a possibility, that they had buried Banaz on the 25th.

The two of them arrived back at Ari Mahmod's property in Wandsworth Road at 20:50 on the 25th. The following day, Hama's car went to Mohammed Ali's address in Brixton and stayed there until 19:30, so there was plenty of time for Banaz to have been buried there as well. Following that, they travelled to Hama's address, then to Wandsworth Road again, where they stayed for just two minutes before heading back to Birmingham. By the time they got to Birmingham it was 23:37 and Omar had been arrested for his public order offence. What on earth were they doing?

But if this was mystifying, what they did over the next couple of days was nothing short of bizarre. On the 27th, they spent the day in Birmingham, then drove back to London in the middle of the night, arriving at 02:02. They went to Brixton for six minutes, then returned to Birmingham. Six minutes! This is a journey of 100 miles each way. The following day they returned to London again.

We searched every mile of that journey, recovering every bit of CCTV evidence that could possibly have shown the suspects looking for possible deposition sites. Harvesting that CCTV evidence resulted in only one positive outcome. At a motorway service station we had an image of Dana Amin's Lexus.

I knew that story he had given on Day 1 was wrong. It would have been so much easier if we had seized the vehicle, but the truth was that he wasn't a suspect at the time. There was absolutely no need for Dana to have turned up at that Wimbledon address and offered to show Richard Vandenburgh the inside of his boot. He had done it out of sheer bravado. By now I understood that women in the community gain respect from what they abstain from doing – theirs is a passive role. In contrast, men gain their respect by taking positive action. By turning up and showing a police officer the boot of his car, Dana was being "manly".

Dana was now a suspect and was duly arrested. Hama had said in his taped conversation that he and Mohammed Ali had not allowed Dana to know the exact place in Birmingham where they buried Banaz, but instead told him they had taken the body to Derby. In interview, when asked about his vehicle being at a motorway service station on the M1, Dana stated he had lent his car to a Kurdish man who had taken it to Derby. Funny, that. According to Dana, the man who had borrowed the car had conveniently now returned to Kurdistan and was unavailable to verify his account. No, he had no forwarding address or contact details.

We didn't have sufficient evidence to charge him at that point and released him on bail. Further inquiries revealed that his bank card had been used to withdraw cash in Birmingham during the relevant period. We brought him in again. Oh, he lent his bank card to somebody else, no surprise there. He was bailed again. This time he left the country and fled to Kurdistan. It was amazing how many men in our inquiry had spontaneously decided to return there.

We read and reread the transcripts of the taped conversations, trying to overlay the information from them against the communications and tracker data. What if this toing and froing between London and Birmingham was them trying to fix the broken water pipe? Working on that hypothesis, we started to concentrate on an area of Birmingham called Handsworth, where the Ford Focus had stopped on several occasions. But how to find the address? All that we knew about the address we were searching for was that some Kurdish men had been staying there, it had a bricked-up window, it was not overlooked from the back and the house next door was derelict.

We looked for addresses with Kurdish connections. We rang the water company to enquire about leaky pipes. We turned over every hypothesis we could think of. We lived and breathed and slept trying to find that address. It consumed my every waking moment. I even thought about it when I was asleep. There were several occasions when an idea occurred to me when I was asleep, so I started leaving a notebook on my bedside. Other nights I would just lie awake, hour after hour. What was I missing? What hadn't I done?

My husband was brilliant. He would offer to get up and make me a cup of tea in the middle of the night. I was barely seeing my youngest two children. My husband had taken over the cooking and washing for a few months. One weekend I thought I would make it up to the kids by taking them to the cinema to see *Pirates of the Caribbean*. I don't think I even got past the opening credits before I was snoring loudly and had to be repeatedly prodded awake. I had developed one of those thousand-yard stares. Where was she? Where was our girl?

Rick, Craigy and Stuart took team after team up to Birmingham looking for the deposition site, creeping round in the wee small hours, following people, watching addresses. One officer, DC Jim Mason, had me in stitches describing how he had to leap over a fence when attacked by a dog in a dark alley. (He still reckons he left a vital part of himself behind on that fence.) West Midlands Police were massively helpful and accommodating, assisting with searches and surveillance. Week after week went by. Anniversaries and children's birthdays were missed. Plenty of interesting people came to our notice; the taped conversations revealed that a Kurdish man living in Birmingham knew the location of the burial site. We placed him under surveillance, hoping that he would lead us to the site. But still no trace of Banaz.

Craigy was a massive sports fan, and he was fond of quoting the Canadian ice hockey player Wayne Gretzky: "You miss 100 per cent of the shots you don't take." That summed up our attitude exactly, and it became the team's mantra. We would try anything. One of the lads gave me a photograph of Gretzky to pin on my wall. I still have it.

In prison, Mohammed Hama and his cronies were getting more confident by the day. They frequently spoke about the fact that the police in the UK were stupid because we didn't torture people like the police in Iraq. These people were all asylum seekers and it was galling to hear them speak in a derisory way about being treated fairly, but it made me even more resolved to see justice. There was absolutely no way on God's earth I was going to let these men get away with murdering that beautiful girl. Brave words, but the truth was that if I didn't find Banaz there was every chance they *would* get away with it, and I was running out of time.

FINDING BANAZ

Handsworth, Birmingham, April 2006

Rick Murphy was running out of time for another reason. His wife was due to give birth to their second child in mid-April. Much as he wanted to, spending days on end away in Birmingham was no longer an option.

On 7 April, Craigy, Stuart and I drove up to Birmingham to meet the crew of the West Midlands Police Air Support Unit. We wanted to fly over the area to see if we could identify the house from the air. We were absolutely confident that we would know this house when we saw it, for, as I have said, we had lived and slept and breathed looking for it for months. Keilly McIntyre had prepared a list of potential addresses for us to look at, but the intelligence was scant to say the least.

Craigy was the natural choice to go up in the helicopter, as Stuart was too heavy and I was scared of flying. He weighed in and put on his flying suit, and the usual mickey taking ensued, as you can imagine, with quotes from *Top Gun* and *Independence Day* flying around. He looked more like a ginger Tinky Winky than Tom Cruise but don't tell him I said so.

Full of optimism, we made our way to the Handsworth area by air and road respectively and started surveying the properties. Craigy was using a piece of camera kit which had the ability to zoom in on objects of interest on the ground, but also to relay live images to me in my vehicle below. One by one we looked at the addresses, looking for properties that were not overlooked from the rear, were next door to a derelict house and had a bricked-up window. There couldn't be too many of those, could there?

Sadly, we came back to London that night with our tails between our legs, because that description fitted any number of houses in Handsworth. A deprived area, it was full of derelict houses. Scores of old Victorian terraces had windows bricked up, outhouses converted. Several addresses on our list had appeared promising from the air, but, once examined at close quarters, they were obviously not what we were looking for. It was a bitter disappointment.

We were back to square one. We knew that our suspects had killed Banaz, we knew we had the right man in custody, but he was going to walk away unless we could find the body in the next month. In desperation, I decided that the only remaining option was to conduct house-to-house enquiries in Handsworth. It would be a hugely resource-intensive operation with absolutely no guarantee of success.

Back we went to West Midlands Police (have I mentioned that they were brilliant?). This time I spoke to Chief Superintendent Steve Jordan. After I explained my problem to him and assured him that the Met would foot the bill, Steve asked me what he could do to help.

"Well," I said, "I need an office to work from, some logistical assistance and a few bobbies." (They call police officers bobbies up there; I thought it was appropriate to use the local lingo.)

"Fair enough," said Jordan. "Go and get yourself a cup of tea and come back in half an hour. I'll see what I can do."

When I returned there were two uniformed chief inspectors and another staff member in his office. "Right," said Steve. "This is Chief Inspector So-and-So – he is your bronze manpower. This is Chief Inspector So-and-So – he is your bronze operations. And this is So-and-So – she is your bronze logistics." (A "bronze" leader is the tactical leader of a particular strand of an investigation.) "We are opening up a disused police station for your sole use. Computers will be up and running by tomorrow. I am giving you twenty officers and I've laid on Force Feeding [refreshments for large-scale policing operations]. Oh, and by the way, you do realise it's a bank holiday that weekend and they will be on double pay?"

Any officer reading this will know how incredibly generous this behaviour was. I had expected a corner of a room, a computer and two constables. The public sector has been bled dry over the years. Even if I was paying the overtime bill, to carve twenty officers out of Jordan's day-to-day operations was a huge ask. I could not get over his level of generosity and I vowed to myself there and then that if I was ever approached for assistance by another force area, I would be as helpful as this man.

I then drove every street in the search area and prioritised them in order of likelihood, before devising a list of questions for the occupants. We were also keeping a man under surveillance who, we assessed from the recordings, knew where the deposition site was. Perhaps our activities might flush him out, drive him to make a move to get rid of the body. To be honest, at that stage I was looking for anything that might give me a lead. It was a desperate last throw of the dice. It was a Wayne Gretzky moment.

Just two days before we were due to commence the house-to-house enquiries, we finally got the breakthrough we so desperately needed. I will remember that moment for the rest of my life.

The latest translation of the covert recordings had been completed and, as usual, we couldn't wait to devour the contents, hoping for a clue. On this occasion, there was a conversation between Mohammed Hama and the very man we suspected of watching the deposition site. As usual, the conversation between the Kurdish men was full of boastful arrogance and self-congratulation – "the police will never find her, they are too stupid" and so forth. Then, the golden moment.

Hama asked his friend, "Did you put the freezer back on top of the patio?"

Hallelujah!

Craigy and I looked at each other.

"We've seen that freezer. Where was it?"

Bear in mind we had searched about fifty addresses by this point, if not more. I closed my eyes and tried to visualise where I had seen it. An image came into my mind of a freezer on a patio and I knew it was on the footage we had taken from the helicopter. After a few minutes of panic, trying to find the video tape in question, we sat and viewed it together. There it was in glorious technicolour: 86 Alexandra Road, Handsworth.

Of all the properties we had looked at this had seemed the least likely. It had a patio made of crazy paving, but it showed no signs of disturbance. Now I understood why – Banaz had been hidden under the freezer.

Craigy, Rick and a couple of others set off immediately for Birmingham with a view to obtaining a warrant. The excitement was palpable. How many times had the boys been back and forth to and from Birmingham and returned empty handed? This time, we felt sure, would be different.

As for me, I was hopping mad because I was halfway through writing a report in an attempt to get permission to use our sensitive intelligence as evidence. I had already tried once and been given a resounding "no", but I had to keep trying. Without confessions or a body, I had no hope of getting past the application to dismiss. It was not something I could delegate to someone else and I was almost crying with frustration.

Later that day I had a phone call from Rick, excited as a kid at Christmas. "This is definitely it," he said. "The house looks abandoned. I've got people watching it overnight. We will get the warrant this evening and be good to go in the morning." Rick had just had his baby girl, and she was only two weeks old. The very last thing he needed was to be spending time away from home, but there was no way he was going to miss this.

Sod the report. With any luck, I wouldn't be needing it now. I jumped on the next train to Birmingham without so much as a change of clothes and was met at New Street station by Craigy. We had a sneaky drive past the plot as he brought me up to speed with the news, then met up with the rest of the team to plan the next day's activities over a beer or two.

It is difficult for me to articulate just how critical it was for me to find Banaz's body. It wasn't just about the evidential significance or bringing the offenders to justice, although clearly those things were hugely important. It was more than that. It was about love, it was about respect. The thought of her being crammed into a suitcase and left to rot in a garden was an abomination to me. We had to recover her body in order that it might be laid to rest with respect and due cere- mony. Respect for the departed is a right that is recognised the world over – even in war people are given licence to recover the bodies of their dead. The overwhelming majority of Banaz's family wanted her to remain hidden – never to be mourned, never to be mentioned, no prayers to be said for her soul, no grave to be remembered by. But she was our girl now, and we wouldn't allow that to happen.

Early the next morning, 27 April, we executed two search warrants, gaining entry via the derelict property next door. It was vitally important to us that nobody knew we were there as we had people on bail all over the country. Some of these were under surveillance, but others were not. We knew that two of the people responsible for killing her had already fled the country and, once the word got out that we were digging up Alexandra Road, there was a strong possibility that others would flee. We were greatly assisted by the fact that it was very difficult to see into the garden of number 86.

We slipped quietly in through the overgrown garden next door and put on our forensic suits and overshoes. I looked around. The scene was exactly as described in the record- ings. To the rear of the house was a steep drop, meaning that it could not be overlooked from behind. The derelict house next door had a boarded-up window but number 86 itself had a bricked-up window facing onto the garden. There was a small lobby area at the back of the house and inside, propped against the wall, we could see a spade.

It was an unseasonably warm day for spring. A sycamore sapling growing in the garden had leaves tightly in bud. The rest of the plot was neglected and unkempt – there was no love here. As we stood and took in the surroundings, my feelings of exhilaration and anticipation began to be tempered by an overwhelming sadness, that a beautiful young woman should have her final resting place in this loveless location. Dandelions were in profusion throughout the garden and to this day I cannot see a dandelion without being transported to that April morning in Handsworth. I can even smell it.

The garden was pretty much unaltered from the video footage. The top quarter was given over to crazy paving. There was no visible sign to me of any disturbance. The house was in the middle of a terrace, along the back of which ran an access path. On the path, between number 86 and the derelict house, someone had placed a huge pile of rubbish which had the effect of preventing anyone from using the path or seeing into the garden of number 86.

There was nothing remarkable about the pile, in and of itself. Discarded supermarket trolleys, stained mattresses and dismantled engines are the hallmark of most low-rent neighbourhoods where people lack the will or means to dispose of such items. In this pile, however, there was a sofa and two armchairs, a small table, and a large freezer with its door missing. There were also several rubbish bags full of household waste. The door of the freezer had been placed under a hedge further down the garden.

In order to examine the scene, we had engaged the services of a forensic archaeologist, Barrie Simpson. As it happens, Barrie was a retired detective superintendent who had investigated a murder or two himself. Archaeology had been a hobby when he was still in the force and when he retired, his hobby became his new career. Because of the sensitivity of our intel, we could not explain to Barrie exactly why it was we suspected Banaz was buried in that garden. We just gave him the usual bland "Our inquiries lead us to believe . . ."

Barrie squatted down on his heels and surveyed the plot. "Well, I can tell there has been soil disturbance straight away because I can see an alluvial flume."

Rick and I were most impressed – apparently this meant he could see where mud had been washed down the patio. We nodded sagely as if we heard the term every day.

Barrie pointed to the freezer door sitting under the hedge. Bear in mind that nobody had mentioned a freezer to him. The door was sitting in a small pile of soil which Barrie could tell was of a different type to that on the surrounding surface of the garden. He explained to us that when a hole is dug in compacted earth – and remember this hole had been dug in the bitter cold of January – the soil which is removed from the hole becomes looser and bulkier. When the time comes to replace that soil, it no longer fits, particularly if something else has been placed in the hole. The soil under the hedge was therefore potentially from the deposition site. Be still my beating heart!

He then looked from the door back towards the house and said that in his opinion the area of soil disturbance was under the freezer. I resisted the urge to kiss the man. Rick and I calmly agreed with Barrie that the most sensible place to start excavating would be under the freezer, our faces giving away nothing of our excitement.

We stood back, making sure not to touch *anything*. One of the reasons I never watch police dramas is that I end up screaming at the television in frustration as cops trample all over the scene, grabbing everything with gay abandon. In reality, the process can take many days. To begin with the scene will be filmed, then photographed, before each item is removed with painstaking care, while any forensic evidence is carefully preserved. Each item will be expertly packaged, sealed and catalogued before moving onto the next.

Our crime scene manager, Calvin Lawson, directed the recovery operation. Rick and I watched as the items of furniture were removed and packaged, one at a time, by the meticulous exhibits officer, DC Mark Randall. Progress seemed to be excruciatingly slow. Bags and bags of household refuse were taken away for later examination. Particular care was taken with the freezer, for we knew that it had been deliberately placed on top of the grave to conceal the site. Plus, it was a great surface for retrieval of evidence. Underneath the freezer was a large sheet of plywood and on the underside of that board were several pieces of chewing gum – all with the potential for harvesting DNA. It looked to be an evidence-rich environment.

Once the ground was cleared we could start the excavation. A tent was erected over the site as further protection from prying eyes. The ground was gridded off and Barrie started digging – not with a ruddy great shovel, you understand, but down on his hands and knees, carefully scraping the soil away with a hand trowel, four inches at a time. Each one of those four-inch samples or cuts had to be packaged separately for later examination – who knew what forensic treasure they held? We soon ran out of containers to put them all in. Calvin came up with the bright idea of buying a load of dustbins and with that we visited every hardware store in a five-mile radius, buying up their stocks of plastic bins. The shopkeepers must not have been able to believe their luck.

Meanwhile, Rick and I were fielding hundreds of telephone calls. If it wasn't the guvnors wanting an update, it was the Witness Protection people worrying about Rahmat's emotional state or the Crown Prosecution Service or Rick's missus wondering when he was coming home. I'll give my husband his due – he is very good at leaving me alone when I am working, he just cracks on in my absence and knows I will ring when I can. I am known to throw my phone across the room in a temper if people call me persistently when I am trying to work, though I obviously couldn't do that in the middle of a crime scene. But Craigy was keeping the team updated, Sarah Raymond was keeping Banaz's sister Bekhal updated. The world and their dog were on tenterhooks.

Deeper crept the hole, four inches at a time, until – bingo! Barrie uncovered a lead pipe. The pipe had been broken and a crude attempt had been made to fix it using waterproof tape. Rick and I made eye contact without giving anything away to Barrie. We were definitely in the right place. Snatches of the covert recordings ran through my head. *The pipe had a joint sticking out and it broke.*

Calmly, Rick and I made our excuses and crept away next door on the pretext of making more calls and visiting the bathroom. We waited until we were out of sight before we allowed ourselves ear-splitting grins.

A few moments later we were back watching Barrie as he attempted to excavate around the broken pipe. All of a sudden, the pipe fractured completely and water gushed everywhere. The water company had to be sent for. They shut off the water supply and set up a standpipe in the street. Next came the fire brigade to pump out our deposition site, which by now had filled with muddy water. There we were, trying to keep the whole thing under wraps, and we now had housewives queuing at the standpipe with saucepans and kettles, two fire engines parked out front and huge hoses snaking through the house next door. Meanwhile, at my meticulously excavated crime scene, all the precious evidence was potentially being pumped out with the flood water.

Several wasted hours later, the water pipe had been bypassed and operations resumed. As I was standing there watching, a breeze caught the tarpaulin we had covering the hole. Just for a second it revealed a length of guttering above the back door. I was transfixed. Had I just seen what I thought I had, or was I imagining it? I asked Calvin to find something to lift the tarpaulin with. There it was, as large as life: "Soora was here." Soora, meaning "red" – Mohammed Hama's nickname.

Down and down went the pit into the earth – still no Banaz. What was going on? Barrie was confident that a hole had been dug there. He could see the demarcation line between the compacted earth and the loosened soil, which told him the exact dimensions of the hole, and he could see that roots had been severed by a sharp edge. What he couldn't see was any signs of a suitcase.

Hours passed as the hole grew ever deeper. It got so deep that Barrie could no longer reach the bottom and he had to dig an access trench from one side. Still no Banaz.

By this time, the leaves of the sycamore sapling were fully unfurled, the abundance and exuberance of new life a stark contrast, almost an act of defiance, to what was happening elsewhere in the garden. The light was fading and the hole was up to Barrie's shoulder. The man had been digging all day and was absolutely exhausted. "I'm sorry," he said, "but there's nothing here."

We were choked. There was a real possibility that the body had been removed. The recordings mentioned digging up the body and burning it. It seemed that we were too late, we had missed her. So close and yet so far. Again, some words from the recordings ran through my head. *She is buried to the height of a man . . . I took it under the house.* We couldn't give up now, not without exhausting every possibility.

We persuaded Barrie to give us just one more hour. One more hour and then we would call it a night and regroup in the morning. Back he went into that hole, now working under the glare of arc lights. The warm spring day had passed into a chilly evening and those of us who were watching rather than digging were feeling the cold. At about half past eight, he called up to us. "It's here, I've found it!"

We peered into the hole and there, just visible at the bottom, was the dim outline of a suitcase. We had found her. Thank you, God.

A range of emotions flooded through me. Euphoria. I was elated, of course I was. I had done my job. We had outwitted those bastards who wanted to erase her from the face of the earth and we were a step closer to justice. I was enormously relieved that they hadn't got away with it yet, but I wasn't nearly as ecstatic as I thought I would be. The whole thing was just too sad.

The next challenge was removing the suitcase from the hole – nowhere near as easy and straightforward as you might imagine. The suitcase was large, heavy and completely water-logged. It covered almost the entire surface area of the hole. In fact, the hole was so small in area that Barrie marvelled at the difficulty the suspects must have had in digging it. There was certainly no margin to get alongside the suitcase in order to remove it. Lastly, there was a strong sucking pressure, caused by the suitcase being in contact with the mud, which prevented it from being easily lifted out of the morass, and we needed to preserve both the suitcase and the soil directly underneath it for forensic evidence.

There was nothing for it but to call back the fire brigade and ask them to extract it with their lifting equipment. We swore them to secrecy. Within an hour or two I watched the suitcase swing above us, suspended above the earth by heavy-duty straps, with water streaming from it. Phone calls were made to open up the mortuary to receive the case with its grisly contents, the crime scene was sealed and the team withdrew, exhausted but relieved.

That night I lay in bed, staring at the ceiling, working things through in my mind. The way I figured it, I thought there was a possibility that the CPS might be able to charge Ari. On the admissible evidence, we had Ari's phones in contact with the other suspects on the morning of the murder. They all came together at Mohammed Hama's house before moving onto Banaz's house. After the murder, Ari, and the two Mohammeds went to the Wandsworth Road address, while Omar Hussain headed straight for Birmingham. Ari called Dana Amin, who met them at Wandsworth Road. Dana and the two Mohammeds then travelled together to Handsworth. Later, the Mohammeds drove the Ford Focus within yards of 86 Alexandra Road. At 3 a.m., I jumped out of bed, wrote out my rationale, and then lay there wishing the hours away.

At roughly 5 a.m., Rick called me on my mobile. "I've been thinking," he said. "I reckon we've got enough to charge Ari."

*   *   *

Over breakfast we divvied up the tasks between the team.
There was plenty to do. Bekhal and Rahmat needed to be
informed in controlled circumstances, likewise the family at
225 Morden Road. We needed to call out a duty pathologist
and arrange a post-mortem examination, and the crime scene
needed completing.

You may have heard the expression "Man plans, God
laughs". Just as we had sent people away on their allotted
tasks, we had a call from one of the West Midlands crime
scene co-ordinators. "Just giving you the heads-up," she said.
"It looks like one of the firefighters has given the nod to the
local paper that we were excavating a body. It's all over the
media." Fuck and double fuck.

Mark Randall, Calvin Lawson, Stuart Reeves and I stayed
on in Birmingham for the post-mortem while Rick Murphy,
Craigy and the rest of the team sped back to London on a
blue light to scoop up the suspects who were still at large.
Mahmod, it turned out, had just arrived home after a trip to
Jordan, bringing with him a wife for Bahman. Her first day in
this country saw her witnessing the arrest of her father-in-
law on suspicion of murdering his daughter.

Dr Peter Ackland was the on-call pathologist that weekend. Having hastily organised some childcare, he met us at
the mortuary. Birmingham Central Mortuary is situated in an
old Victorian building, befitting the sombre business that is
carried out there. It had the same characteristics they always
do: echoey corridors; stainless steel trolleys; gleaming instru-
ments; a damp, cold atmosphere that seems to penetrate
every layer of clothing from the feet upwards; and improba-
bly jolly mortuary managers.

Calvin had organised a mobile X-ray team to attend from
London. Their examination revealed the news we had been

hoping for: there was a body in that suitcase. There was one more step before we opened the case, and that was taping for fibres. Once that was completed, Calvin carefully removed the lid with a scalpel. There inside the case, curled up into the foetal position, was our girl. I cannot describe to you the feeling of heartache I had as I looked on. In my mind's eye, I saw her as she had been in hospital on New Year's Eve. I could hear her dry mouth describing how her father had tried to kill her. I could hear the abandonment and the sorrow as she said the word *"Baba"*, "Dad".

The fact that she was curled up in the foetal position I have always found particularly tragic. I have never been able to articulate why it offended me so, but, to me, there is something about that position that signifies safety and protection. It is the position we humans adopt in times of extreme danger and vulnerability, but more importantly, it is the position we are in while we are carried in our mother's womb, nurtured, protected and loved.

To see Banaz forced into that suitcase by her own family was too cruel for words. I simply do not understand how a parent can depersonalise their child to that extent. I love my children so much it's like a physical pain in my chest. I will never understand how making you look bad in front of your friends could justify murder. It was as if Ari's and Mahmod's daughters were no more than possessions, commodities to be traded, admired or disposed of, a means of boosting one's own status. I felt nothing but anger, loathing and contempt for those men.

I don't intend to go into the details of the post-mortem – I owe Banaz that much privacy at least – but there are a few points which are relevant to the investigation. Everything was exactly as described by Mohammed Hama in the covert recordings. First, Banaz's elbow and hair were sticking out of the suitcase. Second, she was wearing only knickers. Third, around her neck was a long cord, similar to a bootlace. They hadn't even bothered to remove it.

A STRING OF BEADS

Lewisham police station, May 2006

One of the things I loved most about my job was being a voice for the voiceless, redressing the power balance for the victims. It is difficult to articulate but something I feel strongly about, particularly when a person has been murdered with no witnesses. It's a way of saying, "You're not forgotten. I have taken up your cause and I will fight for you."

I hate bullies, and Ari Mahmod was a bully of the first order. Like most bullies he was a coward, good for sending his henchmen to rape and strangle a defenceless girl, but that's all. He was so supremely confident that he was going to walk away with this murder that charging him was an absolute pleasure (I'm only human). Mahmod Mahmod was already in custody at Lewisham police station that day, and I made sure he was present in the custody suite to see his brother get charged. I needed him to know that they were not invincible after all.

I also took pleasure in involving as many women as I could in the charging process. I, the senior investigating officer, was a woman. The Crown prosecutor was a woman.

The family liaison officer protecting Bekhal was a woman. I searched high and low for a female sergeant to do the charging but there were none on duty that day.

I took Keilly McIntyre down to the custody suite to watch Ari being charged. It was a form of reward for her diligence and dedication – most of the support staff never get to see the action. Keilly had worked relentlessly, sleeping in the archive cupboard for days on end. As the charges were read out, the brothers did their best not to look at each other. Ari never showed a flicker of emotion – he only smirked, as if we were boring him.

Keilly raised her hand to high-five me and I responded. It was something we did most days, but it wasn't terribly professional of me to do it in the charge room. I saw a flicker of irritation cross Ari's face and sure enough, a couple of days later a letter from Ari's solicitor came winging in to my detective superintendent, Simon Morgan. The letter complained that I had humiliated Ari in front of his brother. I had affronted his honour, apparently. Craigy and I had known Simon for many years, having worked with him at Carter Street. He was someone I held in the highest regard, a dogged investigator. I explained the circumstances to Simon, who wasn't overly bothered and he provided a suitable response to the brief.

We wanted to record Ari's conversations while he was in custody. The CPS counselled against it in the strongest possible terms – we had already found the body, after all. In the UK, the police and the CPS have a legal obligation to advise the defence about anything which either undermines the prosecution case or assists the defence. This legal obligation is a continuing duty throughout the course of any investigation and exists to ensure that a fair investigation is carried out. Every time we recorded one of his conversations, we ran the risk that he was going to say something we needed to disclose, and the method we were using to record those conversations was so sensitive that it could mean we had to drop the whole prosecution.

While it was true that we didn't need the recordings to find Banaz, the risk to Rahmat and the women in Mahmod's household had gone through the roof. We figured that if anyone was going to give the order for anything to happen to them, it would be Ari, and listening to his conversations was the only way we had of finding out what that might be in time to do anything about it. I made the decision to record him.

Ari didn't disappoint. In a conversation with his brother, he described Banaz as a complete whore. Referring to the innocuous text messages she had sent to Rahmat, he said, "Honestly, brother, if you could read those texts, you would give up everything you have in life, even if it meant that you and your family would die, just to burn her alive if she came back to life."

Burning people alive figured a lot in his conversations. On another occasion, he said that as far as he was concerned none of the Mahmod women was better than the others. They all deserved the same fate as Banaz. The original plan had been to burn Mahmod's house down. Omar had said to Ari, "Just let me pour a barrel of petrol over their house. I wouldn't let even one of them escape."

In another conversation, Ari said Mahmod had come to him the previous October, asking for help to kill his daughter. This was interesting for two reasons. Up to that point we had considered that Ari was probably the driving force behind the murder and Mahmod the weaker of the two. Clearly this was not true. This was not a case of Ari trying to shift the blame

– he was proud of what he had done. But the timing was bizarre, we thought: why October? Banaz and Rahmat were not seen kissing each other until December.

Two things had happened in October. Firstly, Banaz had made her allegation to the police about her husband, Ali Abass Homar. The second thing was that, according to Rahmat, October was when he and Mahmod had spoken in the car. Mahmod had told him he must end the relationship, and Rahmat had called Banaz in front of her father. She had sobbed her heart out and Rahmat had commented to Mahmod, "That is how strong our love is for each other."

Ari said that when his brother had approached him for help, he had given the job to Omar Hussain, who had responded, "Of course. How do you want me to do it, with my hands, with a gun?" Ari had told him: however he pleased.

It made absolute sense. Banaz had left her abusive marriage and made an allegation to the police. She then started a relationship with a man of her own choosing. Her father, already disapproved of within the community as a result of Bekhal defying him, warned Rahmat that the relationship could not continue. He approached Ari for help and Ari outsourced the job to Omar. That explained why the group of men had been following Banaz.

Ari spoke about Mahmod being weak. "He was supposed to have done the job on New Year's Eve, but he let her get away . . . We are in here because of him. She ran away. He pimped for her [allowed her to see Rahmat]. He didn't have the courage to kill her. Brother Mahmod had no courage." He was contemptuous of his brother when he read in Rahmat's statement that Mahmod had kissed Rahmat's hand.

It was Ari's conversation with his wife, Pakiza, that was the most enlightening, for it gave us both motive and timing.

Ari described Banaz as being a whore and a spy, and said, "They came to me at nine o'clock at night. They told me police will arrest all of us tomorrow because she has reported us. It had to be done right there and then. We had to kill her before the appointment. We would all have been arrested and none of us would have known what to say. As it is two of us have escaped and the rest of us know what to say."

Pakiza asked her husband, perfectly reasonably you may think, why, if he knew that Banaz had been to the police, he didn't simply leave her alone – then he wouldn't have had any questions to answer.

"Shut up, you stupid woman," he snapped. "When I talk, you listen. Leave your sentimentality to one side. I am not in here for anything I am ashamed of. I have done justice." He talked about reputation being more than life itself and told his wife that people in the community would be thanking him for what he had done.

Even amid the darkness, there were moments of pure comedy in those transcripts. At one stage, Ari's plan was to throw himself off the top bunk and pretend he had amnesia so he wouldn't have to answer any questions. He asked his brother Johar to go away and research the symptoms of amnesia. The next time they spoke, Ari asked Johar whether he had the results of the research.

"No," said Johar, "I forgot."

Stuart, particularly, loved this passage. You need to have things to laugh at when you are investigating these cases. You would go mad otherwise.

One Kurdish man after another spoke to either Ari or Mohammed Hama, pledging their allegiance and offering to give false evidence in order to get them off at trial. Like Dana, they simply could not wait to get involved. One man was going to say he was using Ari's phone; another would say Mohammed Ali only visited Hama's address to drop off some cigarettes; somebody else would say Rahmat had confessed to killing her. One man would provide a false alibi, say they had seen Ari at the cash and carry; another would say Banaz was angry at Ari and made up stories about him because he wouldn't help her to get a mortgage, and that she also made up stories about her father to get a council house.

One man's feelings were hurt because he hadn't been invited to kill the girl and he asked Ari why he hadn't been included, like a petulant child.

"You are not a man, you are not a man," said Ari.

Always this emphasis on manliness. Always the deference, almost reverence towards Ari, the reference to him as "Agha", an honorific meaning he was considered an important member of the family. Always the reference to Banaz as a "whore". Always the references to honour. One of Banaz's cousins, Johar's son Azad, agreed: "That girl was so low. She deserved it – a man is nothing without honour."

All in all, if you take into consideration the men who had followed Banaz and reported her actions to Ari, the men who planned the murder, the men who murdered her, the men who drove her body to Birmingham, the men who buried her and the men who fell over each other to offer false evidence, more than fifty men were involved in this crime. Fifty. Fifty men to murder one young girl. And they prided themselves on their manliness!

Rahmat had entered the Witness Protection programme in March, when Mohammed Hama was charged with Banaz's murder. He was safe, as long as he stuck to the rules, but there was a determined effort to find him and kill him. In those taped conversations, we listened to suggestions to lure him into a meeting by telling him that everything was forgiven or even offering him money. Once he arrived they would kill him publicly in the market where he worked or in front of his house. Other conversations suggested that if they couldn't kill him or bribe him then they must discredit him – something they continued to try to do for the next few years, without success.

Poor Rahmat. He had arrived in the UK in the back of a lorry. As fellow asylum seekers, Omar Hussain, Mohammed Ali and Mohammed Hama had become his de facto family in the UK. Rahmat had lost the woman he loved and blamed himself for her death. Now, he had to leave the few family members he did have and start a completely new life by going into Witness Protection. He was going to give evidence against the only friends he had in the UK. He knew that they had killed his girlfriend and would kill him too. He was bereaved, furious and ashamed at being in hiding, but for all that, he was resolute. He wanted justice for Banaz and he wasn't going to quit.

Rahmat was not the only one at risk. Banaz's mother Behya was a potential witness, and the recordings made it clear that if she opened her mouth she would be killed. As Ari put it, "Her husband will kill her. If she stays here he will kill her; if she goes back [to Iraq] she will be killed. Tell her this family is a string of beads. If the string breaks, we all go down together."

The other women were in danger, too. We already knew that a group of men had been following the youngest sister to and from school, the same men who had photographed Banaz and Rahmat kissing. Beza's husband made regular contact with Ari in prison. In late May, a woman Bekhal didn't know called her on her mobile phone and asked whether she had had her baby yet. It was as if they were saying, "We are watching you." Bekhal continued to get calls, too, from her sister Payman's husband, Sala Abdullah, trying to persuade her to meet him. Bekhal was scared stiff. Payman herself had already incurred the wrath of other men in the community, who viewed her as a spy because she was the family's point of contact for our family liaison officer. A quiet, respectful and respectable young woman, they wrongly suspected her of providing us with information. Then, also in May, Sala divorced Payman and sent her back to live with her parents. Her reputation in tatters, she had been living at the murder scene, with one of the main suspects.

The risk to all of these people had to be managed. No matter that most of them were refusing to engage with us at all, no matter that we suspected that some of them may have been complicit in the murder. Police have a duty to protect life. But it wasn't just about duty; we genuinely cared for these women. We were becoming too emotionally involved with them, but listening to those conversations and knowing their lives were at risk on a daily basis was harrowing. These women were living on a knife edge every day, always at risk of upsetting one or another man's sensibilities, always at risk of being betrayed by another woman when they had done nothing wrong.

The whole concept was new to me. As someone who was raised in south London – a multicultural city – and having served some twenty-five years in the police by this stage, I thought I knew pretty much what was going on around me. This investigation was a game changer. There was a whole culture that I knew very little about. I had spent several years

working in Child Protection and seen children sexually, physically, emotionally abused or neglected. Each case was a
heartbreaker. But I had never come across this cynical disas-
sociation, this depersonalisation, this hatred. This was a
young woman who, just days before, her family had suppos-
edly loved, and the scale of collusion by the rest of the
community was astounding.

In order to assist us in managing the risk, we engaged the
help of the Violent Crime Command and, in particular, two
outstanding officers: Detective Chief Inspector Gerry
Campbell and Detective Constable Yvonne Rhoden. The
two of them helped us to formally risk-assess each of the
family members and put together bespoke plans. These two
were probably more knowledgeable about honour-based
violence than anyone else in the Met, though they had never
been actively involved in an investigation. There wasn't a
single time I rang them when they didn't respond immediately and willingly. We deployed every weapon in our armoury,
both overt and covert, to ensure those people came to no
harm.

The delivery of those risk management measures fell
almost exclusively on the shoulders of our poor family liaison
officer (FLO), Sarah Raymond. It was far too much work and
responsibility for one detective constable to carry. If there
was one thing I would do differently today it would be the
way I managed that aspect. Sarah didn't get a proper day off
in over eighteen months. To begin with I just lacked experience, but the fact is that there wasn't the centralised support
for FLOs in those days that there is now. I had previously
consulted family liaison advisors and co-ordinators, but more
about methodology where the suspect is a member of the
family. They knew nothing more about honour-based violence

than I did and had little to offer. In terms of resources, I could have asked for another woman FLO from another homicide team, but we were all stretched as it was and requesting a full-time resource for an inquiry which was to last for a number of years is a big ask. No excuses, the fault was mine and I'm sorry for it.

As well as keeping everyone safe, I was also under intense time pressure to solve the murder. The recordings had led us to Banaz's body. Finding her verified their accuracy, but if we couldn't adduce them in evidence at court they were as good as useless. We still had the problem of proving the guilt of the men who we knew were responsible. I badly needed forensic evidence.

CASE FOR THE PROSECUTION

London, May 2006

Sadly, after three months in a watery grave, Banaz's body was at such an advanced stage of decomposition that we were not even able to obtain her own DNA, much less that of the murderers. Neither was it possible to prove evidentially that she had been raped. In the end, we identified her using her dental records.

Firstly we turned to the evidence from the crime scene. Mark Randall, having done an incredible job managing the thousands of exhibits thus far, had done some serious damage to his back lifting those dustbins of soil from the deposition site. He was now off sick and DC Clay O'Neill had taken over the role of exhibits officer. There were 1,700 exhibits from the Alexander Road scene alone, not to mention those from the addresses we had searched and cars we had seized and people we had arrested. Together with Calvin Lawson and the lead scientist, I went through every single exhibit, prioritising what should be submitted for examinations.

We examined every fingerprint on every piece of furniture, we examined the chewing gum on the underside of the board, we examined cigarette butts too numerous to mention – absolutely nothing. We examined the fridge, the lead pipe, the Denzo waterproof tape. Nothing. We did identify a number of illegal immigrants and a man who was wanted for rape, but nothing which would help us solve Banaz's murder. The knickers showed a faint reaction to semen but there were no sperm heads to provide us with DNA. The black tape on the pipe was a bicycle inner tube, but there was nothing on it to identify anybody. We cut away the guttering with the word "Soora" – nothing there either.

Clay took each of the thirty-seven dustbins of soil to our facility at Lippits Hill and put them through a process called wet sieving. Basically, this involves forcing the soil through a fine-mesh sieve with a high-pressure hose, a technique developed following the mass casualties of tsunamis. What you have left is anything that was lying in the soil that is too large to pass through the sieve – fingernails, hairs, cigarettes. We submitted everything for forensic analysis – nothing.

We examined the ligature, my God we examined that ligature, every last bit of it, inside and out. Nothing. We had a knot expert examine the tying of the knot, but nothing useful could be determined from that. It was an unusual knot, not one he had seen before, but that was all. The honest truth is that it's not as easy as it looks on the television.

The hope for forensic evidence to pin the perpetrators to the murder diminished day by day, although there was still a part of me desperate for anything better than just circumstantial evidence. Eventually, I received my final forensics report. We had nothing. Not a sausage.

Just when it seemed as if our luck was running out, we discovered Mahmod's "dirty phone". Up to this point, we weren't sure we had enough evidence to charge him. We had

CASE FOR THE PROSECUTION

plenty of circumstantial evidence – Banaz's video recalling the events on New Year's Eve, Ari's taped conversations – but very little we could adduce in evidence and no "hook" to hang the circumstantial case around. Along with Keilly McIntyre's analysis of the other 300 telephones in the case, we now had evidence of multiple contact between Mahmod and the other suspects at the relevant times. In early August, we charged Mahmod with his daughter's murder.

On the day Mahmod was charged, Rick Murphy and I went to see his wife Behya at their home address, to ask whether she had any further information. I wondered if she would have the courage to speak to me once her husband was safely in custody. It may even have been that she had information which would have prevented her husband from being charged, such as coercion from Ari. I spent some time with her, explaining how we could keep her and her other daughters safe, explaining about Witness Protection.

She wasn't interested. She pulled her headscarf over her head and said, "What can I do? He is my husband. I will say he was with me all morning." She then claimed to have another of her headaches and that was it, conversation over. She had made it very clear where her loyalties lay.

Mahmod was only in custody for a few short weeks before he managed to successfully apply for bail, but it was long enough for us to record some of his conversations. Behya described to him how I had tried to persuade her to give evidence. "Big nose put her arm around me and promised me a new house . . ." They laughed together. Then Behya offered to get him an alibi from an acquaintance of theirs. The alibi was obviously false, as Mahmod counselled her to take care as they didn't know what story the acquaintance might have already told police. He also told her to take care because the police were bugging the phones, which was a bit ironic as we were recording his conversation at that very moment. "That's OK, my husband," replied Behya, "I have a different SIM card for when I contact those guys."

So, here was Behya, who always presented as so unworldly and unwell and who I had thought of as a grieving mother, too afraid to assist police, having separate SIM cards to obtain false alibis for her husband. It's not that I underestimated women as perpetrators – it's more that I did not understand their way of thinking. The thought of a father killing his own child purely for his own reputation was abhorrent, but the concept of a mother being involved in that was completely anathema. I could not and cannot understand how it can be in a woman's interests to commit or enable acts of violence against any other woman, least of all her own daughter, in order to perpetuate a patriarchal society that does not benefit women.

Beza had also been present during that conversation. Mahmod told her she must write a statement at least as long as Bekhal's describing what a loving father he was, how he spoiled his daughters and was never strict with them, how he encouraged them to remove their headscarves.

Knowing more about honour-based abuse now, I understand that "dishonourable" behaviour by a daughter reflects badly on the mother too, as it is she who should have instilled the proper virtues in her daughter. She must now take positive action to redress her own shortcomings. It has been explained to me that people from communities who are affected by honour-based abuse are less focussed on themselves as individuals, and view themselves as part of the wider community. Thus, one daughter may be sacrificed to preserve or restore the honour of the others. I have since researched every known honour killing in the UK. Women have been involved as perpetrators or facilitators in the overwhelming majority of cases.

The trial had been set for 5 November. Time was marching on and I was worried about the strength of the evidence. Without any forensic evidence, I was largely relying on mobile telephone communication data and hearsay.

Circumstantial evidence can be a good thing – in fact, some juries like to do a bit of the detective work themselves, rather than have the whole thing spoon fed – but it needs a hook to hang on. Any experienced detective will tell you that you can't run a trial on mobile phone data. Firstly, it is an inexact science. It can only give you the rough area where the phone was used, and there are many things which can adversely affect the reliability of the data. A bigger problem is attribution of the phones at the relevant time. In our case, Keilly had done an excellent job in providing a report which evidenced attribution, but it is the easiest thing in the world for someone to say it wasn't them using the phone at any relevant time. What was worse was that we knew, from the taped conversations, exactly what lies they all intended to tell about the phone usage. We knew it was coming and we couldn't do anything about it. We could use the recordings neither to prove the defendants' guilt, nor to disprove their lies. It was infuriating.

I knew I had only the slimmest chance of getting any of the hearsay evidence in. Hearsay evidence is something which is said about a defendant, out of their presence and hearing, so that they have no means of responding to it. What I was relying on were the allegations Banaz had made to police, Banaz's letter and that clip of footage from New Year's Eve.

The legislation had changed very recently in relation to hearsay, with the Criminal Justice and Police Act 2005 providing a very few circumstances in which it could be used. I thought there was an outside possibility we might be successful. The trouble was that the legislation was so new it was largely untested in the courts. Worse still, the letter Banaz wrote was what we call multiple hearsay. Banaz had heard those names from somebody else and I couldn't even prove who she had heard them from. The one thing you have to prove more than anything else when trying to adduce hearsay evidence is the reliability of the maker of the statement. What did I have? I had a statement from a serving police officer saying that Banaz was a manipulative liar.

It was obvious what the defence would be. I had two defendants who had fled the UK, so the blame would be put on one or both of them. I had little I could use against Mohammed Hama – neither his car nor his mobile had been in the vicinity of Banaz's home address on the morning of the murder, whereas Omar Hussain's phones had been. Following the murder, Omar had driven straight to Birmingham, where the body had been discovered. He was arrested in the vicinity of the deposition site the day after she was buried there. I could not place Ari or Mahmod at the deposition site. Upon being released from the court, Omar had immediately fled the country, the same day Rahmat reported Banaz missing. A clear indication of guilt if ever there was one.

As for the others, there were too many loopholes to contend with. Banaz's original allegation had been against her husband and she had claimed that men were following her in the street who meant to harm her. In her words, "If anything happens to me, it's them." But Ali Abass Homar had been eliminated from the murder – the detailed account he had provided to police had enabled us to verify his where-abouts at the time of the murder and there was no evidence of collusion between him and the other suspects. The men following Banaz had also been identified and eliminated. Remember – all the defence had to do was sow enough doubt in the minds of the jury, even if it was as simple as naming someone else who could have been responsible. It is for the prosecution to prove that specific people are guilty – not for the defence to prove they are not guilty.

We already knew that various men in the community were coming to court to give false alibis. I worried that Banaz's mother or sisters might be forced to give evidence to support the men. In one of the tapes, Ari had said that Payman must make a statement saying how lovely her uncle was, and Beza must say she heard the front door close, imply-ing that Banaz had gone out to the police station.

I needed to get those taped conversations in evidence. Having already submitted one request in June and been given a resounding "No", I decided to try again. A separate gold group had been set up purely to deal with the issue of the covert material, chaired by the commander of covert policing. I resubmitted my request, setting out the history of the investigation with all of its police failures, the ongoing IPCC inquiry, the calls for a public inquiry. I set out the diffi-culties I could foresee in the forthcoming trial. I pointed out that the Met's homicide prevention strategy had mentioned honour killings and how more should be done to prevent them. It was time to put our money where our mouth was.

More than anything else I talked about the effect that failure to convict these men would have on the community.

Not just Kurds, not just Muslims, but all who are affected by honour-based violence. By now I knew my subject well and it consumed me. I needed to do something to combat this insidious practice. If these men were found not guilty, the whole community would know that men who commit these offences are invincible. What incentive would there then be for a victim to come forward in the future, given that many of them come from places where the police are corrupt or complicit in such offences?

We waited and waited throughout the summer while the trial crept ever nearer. Rick and I attended meeting after meeting at New Scotland Yard, taking Damaris Lakin from the Crown Prosecution Service with us on occasion. Those were not pleasant meetings. Fraught is probably the most polite term I can think of to describe them, as my ambition to use the recordings was diametrically opposed to the agendas of other units. I fully understood their perspective, but I was fighting for our girl and I wasn't going to quit. Ultimately, it would be the decision of the home secretary, but first we needed the support of the commander of covert policing, and we didn't even have that.

I could feel an air of pessimism setting in among the team. When you included our other cases, the workload was relentless – at one point, we dealt with five murders in one twelve-hour period. But if my head went down, so would everybody else's. I started to lobby senior officers and the CPS about extraditing Omar Hussain and Mohammed Ali from Iraq.

The other gold group, chaired by Commander Simon Bray, felt to me like it was preparing for the worst. Commander Bray was trying to ensure that we had contingency plans in place in case the defendants were released and Banaz's sisters went missing. The IPCC had been serving out notices to officers that they were under investigation, though that was suspended until after the trial. A discussion was had about who would be the best "talking head" for the Met, should the verdict go against us.

"How confident are you of a successful verdict?" Commander Bray asked me.

"Very confident, sir," I said with a smile, "always confident, you know me."

I might have had my fingers crossed behind my back at that point.

Months went by before, in October, Rick and I heard that the commander of covert policing, Sean Sawyer, wanted to read the full transcripts of the recordings. This was a sea change. No longer were we getting a flat "no", he was at least going to assess the value of the recordings. I hoped against hope that once he read those boasts about the killing, he would come around to my way of thinking.

On 1 November, Rick and I were summoned to another gold group meeting to discuss the matter. This was a mere four days before the proposed trial date. We trekked up to the Yard full of trepidation. This was it. No sooner had we sat down than we were informed that the commander had granted us permission to use the covert material. We were ecstatic and hugely relieved. We also understood the magnitude of what we had just achieved. This type of material had only ever been used a handful of times in the whole of the country, and never before by the Metropolitan Police. People were going out on a massive limb to allow us to use it and we were profoundly grateful.

We were also aware that there were a few people who were absolutely beside themselves with anger that we were being allowed to use it. Within days I began to hear that some deeply unpleasant things were being said about me at the Yard. I understood why, but that didn't mean I liked it. Detective Superintendent Simon Morgan said to me, "Smudger, your job is just to bring that job home. Get those fuckers convicted. Ignore everything else." He was right. He usually is.

Shortly afterwards we were at the Central Criminal Court explaining to the judge that we wanted to introduce new material and asking for the trial to be put back. A new trial date was set for March 2007 and we were reprieved.

Having the trial pushed back was a positive in as much as trying the three defendants together gave us a far greater chance of success than trying them separately. While the evidence against any one of them might have been only moderate, once aggregated it made a compelling story. It was a massive blow, however, to receive an e-mail from Crispin Aylett, the barrister for the prosecution, advising me that he would not be able to take our case in March, due to a prior commitment. I had worked with him on several successful cases. He was, without doubt, my favourite barrister. I was bereft. Not only did I not know who I would be getting next, but whoever it was would have to get their head round an incredibly complex case.

It is so, so important for a senior investigating officer to be able to work effectively with their barrister. The SIO and team will have been working on a case for months, maybe even years, by the time it comes to court, but it is up to counsel to sell that story to the jury. Firstly, they have to get the facts in evidence and then tell it in a way people will understand.

Some barristers are decidedly easier to work with than others. Personally, I can't bear the kind that adopt a superior air when dealing with officers and fail to take their views into account. We may not have the same expensive education as them, we may not speak as plummy, but we are far from stupid and care a great deal about our investigations.

Because we get closer to the victims than the counsel does, it can often feel as though they are uncaring. Of course, in the majority of cases this is untrue. Our roles are different, it's as simple as that. Still, I much prefer the kind who work with the officers as a team, and Crispin was definitely one of those. At our first Baidland conference, as he pulled a face at our evidence, I had told him, "Now then, Mr Aylett, this is one of those cases where you have to clap your hands and shout, 'I believe in fairies'." He didn't go quite that far, but he was willing to listen, and we were deeply disappointed to be losing him.

Crispin advised me that we were getting Victor Temple QC as lead counsel, with Bobbie Cheema as his junior. Victor, he assured me, had a brain the size of Croydon. Bobbie Cheema's name preceded her. A colleague of mine had worked with her recently. His trial hadn't gone well due to a disclosure error and Bobbie had been scathing, given him a proper dressing down. She sounded fierce and I worried that she would be difficult to work with.

It was, therefore, with some trepidation that I made my first telephone call to her. It quickly became obvious by the questions she was asking that she had read the papers and fully understood the case with all of its complications. I asked if she was available for a meeting.

"What about eight o'clock Sunday morning?" she said.

Rick and I looked at each other with relief.

I met her at the back gate of Lewisham police station that Sunday morning, a rather stern-looking, petite Asian woman. I couldn't have known then that I was about to work with someone I would learn to love and admire so much, but I was certainly glad to have her on my side.

Victor Temple, when we met him, was equally impressive. He was vastly experienced, genial and a pleasure to work with. He had a good sense of humour and a real warmth about him – an absolute gentleman. He is also probably the only person in the world who is more rubbish with IT than me, which made me like him immediately. His idea of cutting and pasting was literally to cut a section from his notes and glue it onto another.

So now we had our prosecution team, and we had the tapes, which meant we had a case to prepare.

THE FUNERAL

Morden, June 2006

The day of Banaz's funeral was absolutely scorching, one of those that makes the sweat run down your back before you have walked ten yards. We had been informed by the family that Banaz was going to be buried at Regent's Park Mosque. The Witness Protection people were very worried that Rahmat might try and turn up despite being warned against it, an action with potentially devastating consequences.

Four of us were going to attend the funeral: me, Rick, Sarah Raymond and Mark Randall. We wanted to attend to pay our respects to Banaz, but we also needed to ensure she was buried with due respect. I had heard whispers that Mahmod was going to have her buried without so much as a prayer being said for her. It was a bastard having him out on bail. I felt deeply resentful that I had had to return Banaz's body to the Mahmods. It had been such a battle to find her. We were her family now, not them. I wrote in my decision log words to the effect that I was "blessed" if I had dug her up out of one hole just to see her dropped unceremoniously into another. For that very reason I made sure I had eyes on the Mahmods that day.

I was wearing quite a thick black trouser suit and head-scarf. I don't wear trousers that often and didn't have anything else suitable. I was absolutely melting. Halfway to Regent's Park the phone rang. The family were not going there at all, they were going to a mosque in Tooting. They had deliberately lied to us to prevent us being present at the funeral. My suspicions were confirmed. We doubled back to Tooting and when we arrived it was obvious that plans had not been made for a funeral – the mosque did not even have the facility to take in bodies. The family had pitched up there with no warning.

They went in for prayers, leaving their daughter's body in the hearse parked in a side road. She might as well have been a carpet or a bag of washing. The four of us stood guard on that car all through prayers in the heat. We looked like guards at the tomb of the unknown warrior.

Eventually the family emerged, bringing an imam with them. He didn't look at all happy and told us that no preparations had been made to say prayers, they had literally just turned up and asked him. There is absolutely no doubt in my mind that it was only our presence that forced the family to hold a funeral.

We all moved off to the cemetery and Banaz's body was lowered into a grave in the Muslim quarter. The men stood to one side, the women to the other. We four officers stood between the two groups and slightly further back, watching with interest. Several of the men, all clones of Mahmod, stared at us with open hatred, and I stared right back with no less loathing. Throughout the day, barely a tear was shed for that sweet girl. A few tears from the women, but I didn't see any real grief there. There was only one person I saw who displayed real grief: Banaz's brother Bahman. He came to the graveside and sank to his knees, sobbing like his heart was breaking. I thought about Bahman crying with Bekhal on a park bench after hitting her over the head with a dumbbell. When I first heard that story, I had felt that Bahman was a young man trapped between cultures, wanting to be westernised but still a prisoner of his community. How many other young men are in the same position?

Once the prayers had been said, the men took turns filling in the grave. I watched them shovelling earth on top of Banaz's coffin in that heat and thought of the three other Kurdish men shovelling earth over her suitcase in the bitter January cold. So much had happened in those six months. The men seemed to be enjoying their task. Once the hole was full they set about treading the soil down to compact it. They took turns to join hands in pairs and stamp on the grave. Some of them were smiling and laughing. It looked to me for all the world as if they were dancing on her grave.

PART TWO

JUSTICE FOR BANAZ

THE PROSECUTION

Central Criminal Court, March 2007

The trial can best be described as a four-month gutter fight. It was held at the Central Criminal Court in the City of London, more commonly known as the Old Bailey. Running trials at the Old Bailey was one of my favourite aspects of my job. I loved being part of the history of that institution, which has seen so many famous trials and infamous criminals pass through its doors. You can feel the sheer weight of the law all round you.

Five men were on trial. Mahmod Mahmod, Ari Mahmod and Mohammed Hama were charged with murder. Pshtwan Hama and Darbaz Rasul, Rahmat's friends who had lied about the threats to kill him, were charged with perverting the course of justice. Two men were missing who should have been charged for Banaz's murder – but Omar Hussain and Mohammed Ali had long since fled the country.

We had prepared for that trial with meticulous care. This was what it had all been for. I knew that case back to front and inside out, but at the end of the day it was all about convincing a jury. Those twelve people, each with their own life story and experiences, prejudices and beliefs, would have to be convinced beyond all reasonable doubt that these men were guilty. Would they even believe that these men could kill a niece, a daughter, for escaping an abusive relationship? Only time would tell.

Having got the authority to use the covert recordings, I compiled an index that would help me immediately pinpoint any particular reference in the fifty-five recorded conversations. I categorised them into themes such as honour, discrediting Rahmat, Omar's involvement, hiding the body. And then I learned it by heart.

It began on 5 March 2007, presided over by His Honour Judge Brian Barker, the common serjeant, the second most senior judge sitting at the Central Criminal Court. As we arrived at court, the pavement was full of protestors, led by the campaigner Diana Nammi from the Iranian and Kurdish Women's Rights Organisation (IKWRO). The group were holding "Justice for Banaz" placards. I offered up a silent prayer that we would get that justice. Nothing is a given at trial. Nothing.

In the first week, Mohammed Hama pleaded guilty. It was his only real option given the content of those recorded conversations. He made the derisory claim in his plea that he had only become involved once the body had been put in the suitcase. Quite how he thought he could get away with that, when we had him confessing to pulling the cord around her neck and stamping on her because she wouldn't die quickly enough, was a little beyond me, but I was pleased to have at least one conviction. The judge would decide the extent of Hama's guilt at a separate hearing once the rest of the trial had been heard. Pshtwan Hama pleaded guilty to perverting the course of justice, but Darbaz Rasul pleaded not guilty, as did Mahmod and Ari.

To strengthen our case against Ari and Mahmod, we applied for permission to tell the jury that Mohammed Hama had pleaded guilty to murder. We also applied to get the hearsay from Banaz in evidence. It was a moving – and damning – testimony of the final months of her life. We had good supporting evidence to show that Banaz was reliable and I e-mailed my various bosses that I was "optimistic as always". My optimism was ill-founded on that score.

As I feared, the defence team played heavily on the fact that the female officer who, unlike me, had actually met Banaz had provided a statement saying that she found her to be manipulative and attention seeking. Thankfully, the video of Banaz on New Year's Eve was allowed in, but we couldn't use the letter, nor her allegations to police that Ari had threatened to kill her. We would have to rely on Rahmat to set the scene and explain to twelve ordinary members of the public why on earth a young woman's father and uncle would want to kill her.

The Crown relied upon just two live, non-police witnesses who actually knew Banaz and the defendants: Rahmat and Bekhal. Just two brave people to speak up for our girl. They were not expert witnesses or professionals, just ordinary people who had come to this country fleeing for their lives, looking for something better. The court building itself was bristling with security in case an attempt was made to get at them. The main suspects might have been in custody, but the taped conversations showed us just how many Kurdish men were desperate to get involved and just how much they wanted Rahmat dead. In the past few weeks, Rahmat's family had been under huge pressure. A brother in Denmark suddenly became extremely ill and it transpired that he had been poisoned, although with what, and by whom, was never established. We were taking no chances.

I have heard a lot of police officers over the years say that once you have got your job to court, you have done your bit and the result is out of your hands. I strongly disagree. I believe in fighting right up to the very end. This is the critical point. You not only need to be able to get all of your valuable evidence in front of a jury in a way they understand, you need to be able to rebut anything the defence may throw at you. The accused are facing life imprisonment. They are going to fight with everything they have got and you must fight even harder, because if they are guilty, they will try every trick in the book. Stuart Reeves, Rick and I sat behind Victor and Bobbie in the courtroom, ready to assist when we could. I opened a new notebook. We were on.

Victor Temple gave his opening speech on 14 March and Rahmat was called to give evidence. He cried as he described his love for Banaz: "I don't think I have ever loved anyone as much as I loved Banaz. She was my first love. She meant the world to me."

Rahmat told the jury that he and Banaz had meant to marry as soon as she could get a divorce from Ali Abass Homar. They had even chosen names for their children. In the dock, Ari and Mahmod could be seen sneering, pleased to see him reduced to tears.

When it came to cross-examination, the defence went all out to attack his credibility. Ari's defence QC, David Lederman, put it to Rahmat that he had never loved Banaz – he was just using her. He was questioned about his immigration status, the inference being he had been trying to get leave to remain. Rahmat staunchly denied that was the case. Mr Lederman produced a tape recording in which Rahmat could be heard telling Sala Abdullah that his relationship with Banaz was over. Rahmat was then heard phoning Banaz and telling her the same thing, saying she meant nothing to him. We were taken aback – it was the first time we had heard that recording. Hearing new evidence at this late point in the case is always startling, to say the least. Rahmat stood firm. He didn't try to deny it was him, but he explained that he had been forced to say those things because Sala had threatened him with violence if he did not. He said the tape only contained half the conversation, and that he had talked to Sala for a long time before he was persuaded to make that call. We called for the tape to be examined, plus any recording equipment it had been made on. (Sure enough, a complete section of the tape had been removed and the tape re-spliced.)

Time after time Rahmat withstood challenges from both defence teams. It was even implied that Banaz's death was the result of a dispute Rahmat had had with Omar Hussain. We had heard many of these plots rehearsed in the taped conversations. Rahmat, of course, had not. Even in relation to telephone calls made and received by him in relation to the various incidents, he was remarkably consistent. Bear in mind that he had not had the same access to the billing data that the defence teams had. Prosecution witnesses get to refresh their memories from the statement they made at the time and that's it. But Rahmat performed under pressure, and he would not be shaken on the facts.

The jury were shown the clip of film that Rahmat had taken on his mobile phone in the hospital on New Year's Eve. I saw one of the jury members look across at the dock and turned to see what she was looking at. Ari and Mahmod were actually sniggering together in the dock while the recording of Mahmod's murdered daughter was being played. I carried on taking notes and kept my head down, praying that their appalling behaviour hadn't been lost on the jury. I find that note taking embeds the facts in my memory, but it also prevents me from staring with contempt at the defendants or laughing with incredulity at their bare-faced lies. My mother always tells me I am an open book, so I take care not to allow myself to be accused of influencing a jury or being disrespectful to the court.

Due to the fact that the hearsay evidence had been ruled inadmissible, Rahmat had been told that he could not tell the jury what Banaz had said to him in relation to Ari's threats. As Rick was walking him back to the witness support suite, Rahmat mentioned that he didn't understand why he couldn't tell the court that Behya, Banaz's mother, had warned him personally that his life was at risk. It was the first we had heard of it and, on the advice of Victor Temple, Rick took a short statement. After legal argument, it was ruled that Rahmat could give this in evidence.

David Lederman was furious – he alleged that there had been collusion between Rahmat and Rick to get the evidence in. He shouted at Rahmat across the courtroom, "It was only after the conversation with Banaz was excluded that you suddenly remembered [what] her mother told you." Rahmat stuck to his guns. The evidence was in.

Mr Lederman's point about the tape was to try to show that Rahmat and Banaz were no longer in a relationship by the time she went missing. Rahmat had explained that, following the incident on New Year's Eve, the pair were only pretending to have ended their relationship. In re-examination, Victor read aloud more of Banaz's texts to Rahmat that had been sent during the relevant period: "Good Morning, my heart . . . all through the 24 hours and every second of the day I think of you . . . the last thing to come to my mind before closing my eyes and the first thing that comes to my mind is you. This morning, as I woke up, I just had a feeling like you're calling my name, I was so excited . . . love you heaps, my shining star."

Once again, Rahmat was in tears.

Bekhal was next up. That young woman was petrified and rightly so. Giving evidence is frightening at the best of times. Even seasoned police officers get butterflies before going into the witness box. You are essentially putting yourself in front of a room full of highly educated professionals trying to make you look like a liar. On top of that, giving evidence against your own family is incredibly difficult. No matter what the crime, at the end of the day that person in the dock is still your family. You have probably lived and laughed and cried together, and the feeling of overwhelming guilt is enough to deter many witnesses from giving evidence, even without knowing that the whole community is looking for you and wants to kill you.

We had arranged screens for Bekhal in court, so that she could not be seen by anyone in the public gallery. She arrived every day dressed in an abaya and a niqab, the full face veil worn by some Muslim women. She hated it with a vengeance, although I do remember sharing one moment of laughter with her, long after the trial, when she was trying to light a much-needed cigarette under her niqab on a particularly windy day. Once in the courtroom, Bekhal removed the veil so that the jury could see her face. You could see members of the jury leaning forwards with interest to hear what she had to say. It was a mainly white jury, most of whom were unlikely to know anyone who wore the veil, and it seemed to hold an air of mystery.

Bekhal spoke in a pronounced south London accent, quite unlike Banaz, who had always spoken in heavily accented English, a byproduct of not mixing outside the family home. Bekhal told the story of why she had ended up in care, the beatings, the abuse, her father spitting in her face for catching her with her head uncovered, calling her a bitch and a whore, Bahman trying to kill her for having a black boyfriend, her cousin hitting her male friend in the face with his crash helmet, Ari saying if she was his daughter she would be ashes by now, her parents sending her audio tapes full of pleas and threats. She was obviously very nervous, but she was excellent.

In relation to daily life she said that she hadn't wanted boyfriends or to do anything wrong, necessarily. "I just wanted to be able to have friends, to give my opinion, very small things that British girls take for granted."

Then came the time for cross-examination. The very first question David Lederman asked her was, "Isn't it true that you have a baby?"

Bekhal literally collapsed with fear and had to be taken from the courtroom. Mr Lederman explained that he was trying to prove that Bekhal had been in touch with some members of her family and that was how he knew, demonstrating that she wasn't in fear of them at all. The judge prevented him from asking further questions about her personal circumstances. The truth was that Bekhal had been in contact with some of her family. She was lonely, and she wanted to be loved. It was simply too much for her to bear and she wanted at least to share the news of her child. Bekhal was frightened that she had let us down, but of course she hadn't.

If the intention had been to scare Bekhal into not giving evidence, the defence team underestimated her. She had lived in fear for years. This was only a continuation of life as she had always known it. She summoned up every ounce of courage and went back into court. They challenged every part of her evidence, making her out to be a drug addict and a thief. They implied that she had been bribed or cajoled into giving evidence by the family liaison officer. Bekhal stood firm: she hadn't known what to say when she was first approached by the police; she hadn't wanted to make allegations only for Banaz to walk back through the door. They tried to portray Mahmod as a loving father, a moderate man who had only wanted the best for his wayward daughter. Bekhal pointed out that she had called the police to keep her safe while she went to the family home to pick up her passport, because she was so afraid of him. She explained that the community had a way of describing the difference between attitudes towards men and women: if you think of a piece of white paper covered in black dots, the black dots represent what a woman cannot do. For men the paper is blank – there are no limits.

When she had finished giving evidence, Bekhal turned to the judge and asked if she could say something to the jury, to which he agreed. "You're probably wondering why I'm wearing this," she said, indicating her niqab. "I don't normally dress like this, but I am going to be looking over my shoulder for the rest of my life."

That evening we searched police records and found that call to the police she had mentioned. The following day we produced the officer who had attended the address, who recalled the incident quite clearly. Defence had also accused Bekhal of lying about Bahman's attempt to kill her. We went and found the young man who had taken her to meet her brother, her boyfriend at the time. He was actually serving a term of imprisonment for theft. He and Bekhal had not spoken for many years.

The poor lad was brought to court in handcuffs, flanked by prison officers. He was totally bewildered, having no idea what he was being produced for. We couldn't tell him for fear of being accused of coaching him; we merely reassured him he was there as a witness, not a suspect. To give him his due, he went into that courtroom full of people and answered every question that was put to him to the best of his ability. You could see his shoulders drop when he found out what it was about. He remembered the incident in question and had actually taken Bekhal to hospital to get her stitches. He also confirmed that her family would have disapproved of her going out with a black man.

Bekhal's and Rahmat's ordeals were now over. Although the two of them had never met each other before, they would spend the next four months watching the trial by CCTV link, in a tiny room off the witness service waiting room at the Old Bailey, hoping that their evidence would be enough. They had literally staked their lives on it.

The rest was up to us.

One by one, police officers got into the witness box to give evidence and be challenged by the defence. PC Stephen Hall, the first uniformed officer to attend the home address after Banaz had been reported missing, spoke of the men in the household trying to distract him while he was searching. He commented that the women were not allowed to speak to him. Another officer gave evidence of Mahmod saying he had seen Banaz on the morning of 24 January dressed in T-shirt and jeans; a third described Mahmod giving a different account, saying he had not seen her that morning. A fourth said Mahmod claimed to have seen Banaz go out that morning. None of it quite added up, especially by contrast to the consistency of Rahmat's evidence.

Again and again I passed notes to Bobbie Cheema, on paper torn from my notebook, pointing out pieces of evidence we needed to cover or questions to ask. I have had counsel get decidedly ratty with me when I do that. I can practically feel the irritation radiating out of the back of their gown! Not Bobbie. She took each note with good grace, patiently read the contents and converted it into material for Victor Temple to work with.

A psychiatrist gave evidence of the fact that Banaz had taken an overdose of anti-depressants and tried to hang herself with a scarf in the summer of 2005. She had reported to him that men were following her in the street who meant to do her harm. He was clear that Banaz was not delusional. The ambulance drivers and nurses came and spoke about how frightened Banaz was on New Year's Eve. One said that, when she discharged herself from the hospital, Banaz had confided her catch-22: if I run away I'm dead; if I go home I'm dead. She seemed resigned to her fate. Another medical professional described how Mahmod had turned aggressive when she refused to tell him where Banaz was. The café owner testified that Banaz "was trying to get someone to take her seriously, but nobody did. The female officer was dismissive." The defence tried again to suggest that Sarah Raymond, the family liaison officer, had bribed Bekhal with mobile phones and housing. But Sarah was a consummate professional: every purchase was authorised and recorded by me;

every single conversation was meticulously recorded in thirty books of family liaison logs. The defence scored no points there.

Telephone evidence can be horribly dry. It's a great pity, because it is pivotal to most trials, but if you can't sell it to the jury you may as well not have it. That is why all the pre-trial preparation is so important. Victor Temple didn't favour a graphic representation, so we decided to put Keilly McIntyre in the witness box. She had produced an excellent report detailing the mobile phone evidence we had used. Keilly had never even been in a courtroom, much less in a witness box, and as she stood waiting outside court, she was pouring Rescue Remedy into her mouth like a person dying of thirst.

We deliberately did not coach Keilly in the art of giving evidence, other than to say, "Take your time, stick to the facts and don't let them rattle you." I watched her setting out her books around her in the witness box before taking the oath. Mr Lederman's junior counsel thought he was onto a winner. He, too, had studied the data and tried to steamroller someone he thought was going to be a weak link. But Keilly knew her subject inside out and back to front. Every point counsel made she had an answer for, and then some. Because she had no training in giving evidence her answers came across as refreshingly straightforward and honest. Defence counsel quickly realised he was conceding one bad point after another and sat down – "No further questions, my lord, thank you."

There was a marked difference in the styles of the two main defence teams. Mahmod's QC, Henry Grunwald, challenged every point robustly and had clearly done his homework, but he was professional in the way he went about his business and was never underhand or overbearing. He was a gentleman. David Lederman, on the other hand, had clearly opted for a more confrontational approach. It was Mr Grunwald who worried me more out of the pair of them. Bullies I can handle – it's the quiet ones you have to watch.

Mr Grunwald asked for Rahmat to be recalled yet again. There was a point he wanted to get in. The officer who had dealt with Banaz on 23 January, PC Alison Way, had stated that Banaz had told her she felt safe to go home because her mother was there. Mr Grunwald put it to Rahmat that when Banaz called him that night she said that he, Rahmat, was in danger, but she herself felt safe. Remember the text? "Jus be careful, Rahmat, gian, cus I dnt fink I cud live a second widout u." Rahmat was adamant that Banaz had never told him that she felt safe. It was just typical of her nature – she put his safety even before her own.

THE DEFENCE

Ari and Mahmod chose to speak in their own defence. Both brothers used an interpreter, although neither of them needed one. Knowing that they could speak English fluently, I suspected that this was just to give them time to think.

Before either gave evidence, David Lederman addressed the court on the matter of the tape recording of Rahmat apparently breaking up with Banaz. Our examination had revealed that parts of it had clearly been deleted, just as Rahmat had claimed. Mr Lederman explained that Payman's ex-husband Sala Abdullah, who had made the recording, had had the tape recorder in his pocket. Somehow, by mistake, he had deleted part of the tape where they had been discussing Rahmat's relationship with Banaz, a conversation which had become increasingly threatening. Mr Lederman claimed that Sala had not realised he had deleted the parts of the conversation that corroborated Rahmat's account and had not meant to mislead the court. The whole account sounded ridiculous.

Mahmod started off well as he was led through his evidence by Henry Grunwald. He was smiley and pleasant.

Mahmod described himself as being like a friend to his daughters. They were free to come and go as they pleased and Banaz often spent the night with Rahmat, he said. He produced a few photographs of Bekhal without a hijab, all of which showed her indoors at the house with no males present. I suppose he gambled on a largely white jury not knowing the relevance of that. He would never harm his children, he said: "If I knew my hand was betraying them I would cut it off with my other hand." Apparently Mahmod's father had taught him that there was no difference between boys and girls, nor was there a head of the family – they all consulted each other. In the dock, Ari was visibly amused.

Mahmod claimed to have been happy that Banaz wanted to marry Rahmat. He admitted to having had a two-hour conversation with Rahmat in relation to Banaz. He had only advised Rahmat that he needed to wait until her divorce was finalised. The meeting had ended with Rahmat's overwhelming gratitude, he said. In relation to Banaz's text messages showing that he had threatened her, or was keeping her in the house, he said he had just been giving her loving fatherly advice. It was all a simple misunderstanding. He hadn't wanted her to go out one time, because he knew men were following her. He was trying to protect her. This would be one of the points where I had to take notes.

On New Year's Eve, Mahmod said, he had been at his daughter Payman's house when he found out Banaz was in hospital. Mahmod and Behya had visited their daughter and he claimed that she was delighted to see them. However, when he returned to the hospital the next day, she was gone. His explanation for her disappearance was that she was embarrassed by her bad behaviour. He emphasised that Banaz had returned home after the meeting at McDonald's, and claimed that a couple of days later Banaz confided in Payman that she had made the whole thing up to get a council house.

In order to account for phone calls between himself and Ari at the relevant times, Mahmod claimed that his cousin Hassan had borrowed Ari's phones, and that Mahmod had been calling at various times to arrange for Hassan to come and paint his son's bedroom. In order to refute Bekhal's evidence about Mahmod being a racist, Mahmod called his next-door neighbour, a black woman, to give character evidence on his behalf, to say what a nice man he was. Poor woman, I bet she wouldn't have done that if she had heard the tapes we had, where black people were referred to as cockroaches.

In cross-examination, Victor Temple was nothing short of masterful. Quietly spoken, he took his time when probing Mahmod's answers. It didn't take long for Mahmod to dissemble. He denied calling Bekhal a whore – his tape to her was loving and caring. He also denied threatening to burn her mother and sisters alive. He stated that Bekhal was lying, but instead of leaving it there, he started to get overconfident. "Did she keep a copy?" he asked Victor, in reply to one question. "She would have kept a copy of the tape if it was true. It doesn't exist, therefore it isn't true."

Victor asked him to read aloud from the Social Services record which held a contemporaneous transcript of the tape, word for word. He had no answer for that.

Neither did he have an answer for why Bekhal needed a police officer with her when she came to collect her passport. He said he didn't ask why. "It could have been for another reason," he said, as if daughters often needed police officers to help them collect their property from the family home. The point was not lost on the jury.

Victor put it to Mahmod that he had sent Banaz back to live in an abusive relationship. Mahmod completely denied knowing that Ali Abass Homar had raped Banaz. "I know the relationship had some minor difficulties," he said.

Satisfied for the moment, Victor turned to another point. He asked Mahmod about telephone calls. Mahmod agreed that Rahmat had called him on the night of the 22nd and accused him of trying to murder him. He had no idea why Rahmat would think such a thing. Rahmat had been angry and demanded Ari's phone number but Mahmod had refused to give it, thinking it was bad manners to do so. He hadn't thought to mention this phone call to Banaz, apparently. Victor asked him why not. Mahmod had no answer. Clearly, he hadn't found anything out of the ordinary in being accused of attempted murder.

Mahmod was asked about his relationship with Omar Hussain and initially said he had no contact with him. When asked to account for telephone calls between himself and Omar at critical times he then changed his mind. Omar had wanted to marry Banaz, he said, and someone had texted Omar's number to him so that he could speak to him about that. Mahmod was just making stuff up as he went along, and it showed. Victor had him on the back foot and Mahmod started to show his true colours, becoming angry and raising his voice: "Your question is not sensible . . . That has no basis . . . You don't have any evidence . . . That is an empty allegation . . . They are implicating me because they cannot catch who did it."

He prevaricated and then outright refused to answer. Again and again he was asked by Victor and the judge to answer the questions, and again and again he could not answer them. In relation to the alleged attempted murder on

New Year's Eve, one of his answers was that he viewed the UK as the "mother of democracy". He denied taking Banaz's phone from her. He had no answer for why her mobile was switched off at the relevant time, exactly as Banaz had claimed in her transcript. Neither could he explain why she had no phone, shoes or clothes when she was taken to hospital. Victor challenged Mahmod's version of events in which Banaz had been delighted to see him at the hospital. When confronted by incontrovertible evidence, Mahmod eventually admitted that the nursing staff had asked him to leave at Banaz's request. His explanation was that Banaz was embarrassed by her behaviour.

Victor moved onto another point. He asked Mahmod whether he had known that Banaz had an appointment at the police station. Mahmod agreed that he had, but hadn't known what the appointment was about. Taking his cue from Mr Grunwald, Mahmod couldn't resist dropping in that Banaz had told PC Alison Way she felt safe at home. He hadn't even been asked that question, he simply couldn't stop himself from trying to score a point. Victor did not immediately pursue it, but instead continued with his line of questioning. When asked if he had told Ari about the appointment, Mahmod was sarcastic. "I didn't know he was a police station receptionist." He was making himself look worse by the second.

Victor Temple didn't so much as raise an eyebrow. He returned to the phone evidence. "Why did you call Ari at 09:55 on the morning of the 24th?"

Mahmod became angry again. He repeated his story about Hassan having the phone and Victor put it to him that both he and Ari had concocted that story to account for the calls between them and the murderers.

"You and your team have spent a year trying to set me up,"
Mahmod replied. "You don't have any evidence."

Victor turned to the covert recording of Mahmod's conversation with his wife, Behya, and eldest daughter, Beza, and
read the transcript:

> Behya: I must call Hassan.
> Mahmod: Not on the phone.
> Behya: I have another SIM . . . I will arrange a meet-
> ing through another SIM card.
> Mahmod: Tell him about the arrangement to carry out
> work. Tell him to say, "I stayed at Ari's house to get
> there early in the morning but got another job." He
> must say he went to my mother's house. If that can
> be put in order it will fix matters very much.

Victor put it to Mahmod that this conversation was him and
Behya conspiring to get a false statement from Hassan to account
for the calls between him and Ari on the morning of the murder.

Mahmod said that his wife was crazy and took tablets for
depression, he was only reminding her of the facts. Was it a
coincidence, then, asked Victor, that Ari was also making the
same request of Hassan at the same time? Mahmod had no
answer.

Victor asked him about a comment he had made in the
same conversation, this time to Beza: "Write that we are sure
Banaz was loved." Why did he need to tell Beza that? Was
Beza also crazy? Victor put it to Mahmod that he was telling
his witnesses what to say. Mahmod avoided the question,
replying instead that if his daughters didn't love him they
wouldn't have visited him in prison. It was pointed out to him
that Beza was the only daughter to do so.

Having dealt with that matter, Victor returned to the comments Mahmod had made about the conversation with PC Way. In making those comments, Mahmod had made a grave error. PC Way's evidence had thus far been excluded on the grounds of hearsay, but now that Mahmod had used it, Victor applied again to get it adduced in evidence in order to correct a wrongful impression.

PC Way's statement contained material that was seriously damaging to both Mahmod's and Ari's cases, as Banaz had recounted the whole sorry story to her. Mr Lederman successfully fought to keep out anything that pertained to Ari, but we were able to get in the fact that Banaz had only said that she felt safe at the family home *because her mother was there*. It also corrected another lie told by Mahmod that day, that he hadn't known about Ali Abass Homar raping his daughter. In fact, they had held a family meeting about it. Banaz had said, "In front of my whole family we discussed how he had raped me. [Ali] said that I said no every time, but I didn't because there must have been times when I wasn't on my period and he ripped my clothes off and raped me . . . My family brainwashed me that it would bring shame on my family if I left him and I had to go back."

The following day this was put to Mahmod. He denied again knowing about the rape, but his lies rang emptier now.

Reza came to court to give evidence on behalf of her father. Yes, he was loving and tolerant, the perfect father. Exactly what she had been told to say by her father. In cross-examination, Victor asked her about what had happened on the morning of the murder. Beza trotted out the usual account of being upstairs feeding the baby and having a bath. She mentioned that her parents had phoned her while they were taking their youngest daughter to school.

"What did they phone you about?" asked Victor.

"They were checking Banaz was up because she had an appointment at the police station," said Beza. "They also asked me how I was." She said they often called her if they went out, just to see how she was, even though they had only seen her an hour before.

"Why would they ask *you* how Banaz was, why not ask Banaz herself?"

Beza had no answer for that one.

"Why didn't they ring Banaz's mobile, or the landline in the room where she was sleeping?"

No answer.

We produced records of Beza's telephone calls. It was usual for her mother to ring her once a day. On the morning of the murder, there was a whole page full of calls. Some were from Mahmod, some from Behya, clearly showing they were not together. There wasn't a single call to Banaz from either of them.

"What was said on all of these calls, just minutes apart?" asked Victor. "They couldn't have all been asking you how you were."

Beza had no answer. The members of the jury looked at each other in amazement and several of them exclaimed out loud.

I'll leave it to you to imagine what was being said in those many, many phone calls to Beza on the morning of the murder, while Banaz was being raped and strangled downstairs. I'll leave it to you to decide why nobody called Banaz.

The defence obviously decided not to put forward any other family members after that. From Behya we heard nothing. Maybe she had a headache.

*   *   *

Next, it was Ari's turn to give evidence. He also tried to portray himself as the perfect father and uncle, but had a far more difficult time, largely due to the words that came out of his mouth in the taped conversations. Initially he was totally dismissive of the allegations. But he was unable to keep up the benign-father act for very long and reverted to his arrogant, sneering self. He was hateful, constantly making childish retorts. He denied knowing about Bekhal being followed, denied the family meeting in her bedroom where he had threatened her. "Did she record it?" Ari asked, challenging Victor to prove the allegation. "That is a silly allegation, for four uncles to punish a girl for smoking."

He claimed that Bekhal had been persuaded by police to make allegations against him. Ari's main problem was always his ego. He had to prove that he was cleverer than everyone else, more powerful. Again, I could see it wasn't lost on the jury and I was loving every second of it. Pretty soon that arrogance was the undoing of him.

Exactly like his brother before him, he made a statement in relation to Banaz's appointment at the police station on 23 January which was a blatant lie. He denied that Banaz had made any allegations against him on that date. It was a deliberate, disingenuous attempt to mislead the jury. What was he thinking? Even having seen his brother come unstuck for lying about the same thing a few days earlier and having seen how David Lederman had fought to keep any mention of him out of evidence, he just couldn't help himself.

A lengthy legal argument ensued, resulting in the whole of PC Alison Way's statement being admitted. Banaz had told her, among other things, that Ari had brainwashed the family; that Bekhal had wanted to come home but Ari wouldn't let her as she had brought shame on the family; that she, Banaz, had been seen kissing Rahmat at Morden, which was then reported to Ari; that Ari had called her mother and told her Banaz and Rahmat would be killed. Banaz had also told Alison Way about the events of New Year's Eve. Ari's name and guilt were writ large all over that document.

As it was read out in court I risked a look at the jury under my fringe. You could see the understanding dawning in their faces. This wasn't something the police were plucking out of the air – this girl had been fighting for her life. It wasn't only Bekhal who was saying these things about her father and uncle. Banaz had made similar allegations and now she was dead.

It was put to Ari that he had purposely misled the jury. At first he tried to say he had been referring to a different document, one in which he was not mentioned. Victor found the document Ari was referring to and read it aloud: "My uncle has brainwashed my family and seems to be in control of every decision my father makes." After being repeatedly pressed for an answer by both Victor and the judge, Ari replied that he hadn't had his glasses on when he read that document!

Victor then asked him about New Year's Eve. Ari became aggressive and started raising his voice, making sarcastic remarks.

"You are playing for time because the questions are too hard," Victor replied.

Having shown Ari to be a complete liar, Victor moved on to the phone evidence. Ari squirmed. At first he said the phone was his wife's, then he said it was Hassan's. Victor pointed out that the phone had been seized from his house and the SIM card had "ARI 2" written on it. That phone had been used to call his wife, his daughter, his brothers, business associates, Omar Hussain, Mohammed Ali, Mohammed Hama, Dana Amin and many, many others.

Ari's explanation was that Hassan had been making business calls on his behalf.

"Why, then," asked Victor, "does Hassan call your brother Mahmod sixteen times? Why is Hassan calling your daughter? Your wife?"

Ari had no answers. He started dissembling: he was not a telephone expert, he had never been to court before, he hadn't slept properly. One feeble excuse came out after another.

Victor read aloud the transcript of one of Ari's recorded conversations, in which he was speaking to his brother Johar. In it, they were discussing the telephone evidence.

> Ari: They were both with me.
> Johar: If these phone calls were removed from you . . .
> Ari: Then we can make the jury believe . . .

Ari denied the conversation was anything to do with phone calls.

In another recorded conversation Ari could be heard telling his brother the killing took place on the 24th. They were concocting an alibi that he had been at the cash and carry without his phone. Victor reminded Ari that when he was giving evidence previously, he had said he didn't know when Banaz went missing. How was it that he knew, when he was in prison, exactly when the killing took place? Ari replied that he must have read it in the bundle of evidence that the prosecution had provided to his solicitors. No, said Victor, when the paperwork was served, the prosecution hadn't known when Banaz went missing. The transcript of Ari's conversation also said she was *killed* on the morning of the 24th. That was something only someone who had been involved would know.

Ari admitted Rahmat had called him on the 23rd – he didn't have much option as the call data showed the call. Apparently Rahmat just wanted to know if Ari had a problem with him, to which Ari had replied, "I don't even know you." Victor pointed out that the conversation lasted twenty-seven minutes. Ari then said Rahmat was asking him for a job. Victor then read aloud the transcript of Ari asking Johar to research the symptoms of amnesia so that he could feign it if the questioning got too hard. By this point, even the judge was getting exasperated. Ari had no answers. Eventually he claimed to have a mental health issue.

Victor asked why Mohammed Hama's Ford Focus was parked outside Ari's Wandsworth Road property for the whole of 25 January. Ari said he must have been buying spare parts for his car. It was pointed out to him that Hama's car was a hire car.

When Ari was rearrested on 29 April, copies of statements were found in his car, purportedly written by Darbaz and Pshtwan, stating that no threats had taken place. When asked why these false statements were found there, Ari said they had been on the photocopier in his shop and he had picked them up by mistake with his tax forms. The jury had already heard evidence from Darbaz to the effect that Alan Hama had brought these statements, already written, to the shop where he worked and demanded that he sign. He had signed out of fear of Omar Hussain. It was obvious that this had been orchestrated by Ari.

In the next transcript, Ari was quoted as saying, "There was no other solution. We had to kill her before the appointment." Ari now started to look for a scapegoat. To begin with he claimed he was just repeating something that Omar had told him. Then it changed: someone had overheard Omar saying this on the phone. His contrived explanation was that Rahmat and Omar had conspired together to implicate Ari. Banaz was the victim of a conflict between these two. Now they were blaming Ari, probably out of jealousy because he was so successful.

Why hadn't he told the police this? asked Victor. Had he told his solicitor? Anyone? Ari said he had not commented in interview due to stress. The police didn't give him a chance. They were abusive. He was too upset. He was confused. Ari Mahmod, who had been so arrogant on arrest, was now claiming to have been bullied by police. He even brought up my high five with Keilly as an example of what a bully I was.

The transcripts kept coming. In June he was heard saying, "We will blame everything on Omar. Tell Saleh [Mohammed Ali] to give him £10K. Tell him to say those people in prison had nothing to do with it. Tell Rahmat to write to Mahmod, implicating Omar. Say Omar wanted her for himself." Johar can be heard to ask "Did he?" "No," Ari replies, "we are just saying that." Later, in October, once he had been given the telephone evidence to read, Ari discovered that Omar had telephoned Ari from outside Banaz's house. His response, which we also heard, was, "That dumbass phoned me outside . . . This is a disaster for me. He phoned my home number. Omar's hands have been pushed into the mud . . . It could change the whole case."

REASONABLE DOUBT

Those transcripts were horribly damaging and I could see the jury drinking it all in. Seeing that things were not going his way, Ari tried to say that we had misheard or misinterpreted what he was saying, largely because we didn't understand his cultural background, playing the race card. He claimed that all of the interpreters were mistaken, even his own. He had not said that his brother had asked him for help to kill his daughter, his brother was asking him to kill a goat for Eid. They weren't sacrificing Banaz, they were sacrificing a goat in honour of his dead father. Omar was just asking how the goat should be killed; he was a cultural expert on these matters. Ari argued every point in the same way.

The defence interpreter was called to give evidence. He had agreed with the prosecution interpreters before the trial, so what had happened since? The defence interpreter claimed to have been mistaken. Now he had spent time with Ari Agha, he realised his errors. Ari Agha had made a few alterations. It was all to do with local accents, he said. I noticed that the interpreter was using the honorific title "Agha" – Ari was his superior and he was paying him respect. We then had a royal battle of the interpreters on our hands, with our three interpreters claiming one thing and his another.

Any number of cronies came to give evidence on Ari's behalf. My favourite was the painter and decorator who started off on the wrong foot by giving a story about building a porch for Mahmod, instead of painting Bahman's bedroom. He couldn't remember anything about the job. He couldn't even remember the address or where the house was. Stuart Reeves produced a photograph that showed Mahmod already had a porch. It was donkey's years old and not the best workmanship in the world. Was he saying he had built that? Oh yes, the witness remembered now, the job got cancelled. He had caught Ari's amnesia. But he did have one thing clear in his mind: he was with Hassan on the morning of the 24th and heard him talking to Mahmod on Ari's phone. He was such a hopeless witness that we might as well have called him for the prosecution.

Ari's daughter Ala also came to give evidence on behalf of her father. She was dressed in a leopard-print top which showed her cleavage. She stated her father allowed her to dress however she pleased and she could have as many boyfriends as she wanted. She painted her father as loving and liberal, someone who wouldn't harm a soul. It would have been a comedic performance if the whole thing wasn't so sad. She knew he was guilty, but she was just trying to save her father from going to prison.

Thus far I had avoided using Ala's incriminating MSN conversation with her cousin. It would have been extremely useful, but with the recordings I felt I had enough already and didn't want to put her at risk unnecessarily. Now that she had put her head above the parapet and told a pack of lies, I reconsidered the position. I discussed it at length with Bobbie Cheema. We had to balance the needs of the prosecution with Ala's right to life. The factor that swung in favour of using it was that, by now, Ala had confessed to Ari that the conversation existed and that police knew about it. We had learned this from one of the taped conversations. Ari had gone ballistic when he found out, accusing her of being a spy, no better than Banaz.

So now we used it. Defence fought for time. They wanted to question the cousin about the MSN conversation but couldn't find her. The judge told David Lederman that he should have planned better. Mr Lederman fought to keep it out of evidence on the basis that it hadn't been shown to them in pre-trial disclosure. It took DC Andy Mumford, our disclosure officer, a matter of seconds to prove that it had been.

Ala again tried to dismiss it as nothing more than a joke. She was arrogant, sarcastic and repeatedly rude to counsel. It was very obvious to all that she was lying, and lying badly. She had done her father no favours. It gave me no pleasure to watch Ala being hoisted by her own petard, but I was relieved to be able to set the record straight. All trials are tiring, but this was nothing short of exhausting. Every day we were at full stretch mentally, countering their lies. Every night we went back and conducted further research and enquiries to prepare for the following day. This went on, day after day, for four months.

The play was going against the Mahmod brothers. I could feel the tide turning and so could they. Then, one day, an anonymous letter arrived at court, hand delivered and addressed to the judge. In the interests of justice, it claimed, the writer needed to tell the judge some urgent fact which proved the Mahmods' innocence. The writer claimed that Rahmat had confessed to the killing, following a dispute with Omar over who was going to marry Banaz.

The matter had to be investigated. Curiously, we thought, the letter was written on a page torn from a counsel's legal notepad – not something most Kurdish men had readily to hand. We looked at the CCTV and saw the note being delivered by a small man whose face was covered by a hood. We traced his journey onwards to an Underground station where we lost him. Rahmat was called back into court and questioned about the contents of the letter. Naturally, he knew nothing about it and his bewilderment was very obviously genuine. As the letter couldn't be verified, it carried no weight, but it was yet another crude attempt to derail the prosecution and sow doubt in the minds of the jury. Remember, the defence do not have to prove their innocence; the prosecution have to prove guilt, beyond all reasonable doubt.

The officer who had dealt with Banaz on New Year's Eve was called for the defence. I had avoided her outside the courtroom, but one of my team told me she had been moaning about the fact that her colleagues blamed her for Banaz's death. She had been served with a notice advising her that she was formally under investigation by the Independent Police Complaints Commission.

In the witness box, she denied that Banaz had ever alleged to her or in front of her that her father had tried to kill her. She stuck to her story about Banaz being melodramatic. When asked in cross-examination why a guard had been placed with Banaz at hospital, she replied that she thought it was because Banaz was a danger to the public!

I wasn't allowed into the courtroom to hear her give evidence. The following day, something very bizarre happened. I arrived at court in the morning to find Victor Temple and Bobbie Cheema acting very strangely towards me. They said they couldn't speak to me. I didn't like the sound of that at all, but didn't realise what had happened until I was contacted by the Department of Professional Standards (DPS), who deal with complaints against police.

The officer had alleged, under oath, that I had tried to make her change her statement. She didn't say I ordered her, just that I told her to and she was too frightened of me to say no. Well, she hadn't altered the statement so she clearly wasn't that frightened. But apart from that, she knew me. She had worked for me previously and she would know, as well as anyone who worked for me, that I am as relaxed a guvnor as you are likely to find anywhere. Not only had she failed Banaz on the night in question, she was now apparently content to see the whole trial collapse.

A senior officer from the DPS came to see me at the Old Bailey. Without even knowing the details of her allegation, I readily gave them an account of my dealings with the officer. Yes, I had queried her statement – it was completely at odds with the evidence of every single other witness who saw Banaz that night. Of course I had asked her about it. I was trying to establish the facts, particularly in relation to Mahmod. I had also commented on the quality of the statement because it was so abysmal. She was a specially trained statement taker and should have known better than to fill her statement with pejorative comments and emotive statements that were not based on evidence. I was both fuming and terrified that all our hard work would be for nothing. These cruel men would get off with murdering that girl simply

because one police officer was too stiff necked to admit she
had made a mistake.

I was warned that the press were outside the court building waiting to doorstep me. Victor suggested I use the rear
entrance but I wasn't going to slink out of that building. I
walked out the front, head high, into the wind tunnel that
always seems to whistle up Old Bailey and a barrage of waiting photographers. My picture was all over the paper next
day. I was awfully glad my dear old Mum was on holiday. I
looked absolutely haggard in that photo.

Three agonising weeks went by before I had my opportunity to get in the witness box and explain my version of events
to the court. Weeks of the jury potentially thinking I was
dishonest, that any of the evidence I was putting forward
lacked integrity. I used to walk down the road to the railway
station in the morning dreading going into court. I wished I
could stay on the train, keep going, anything but go in there.
But go in I did, always with a big smile, always courteous,
always calm. I am a great believer in grace under pressure.

One of the things that worried me was how I could answer
the inevitable question of why the officer had made that allegation against me. I wanted to get in there and say she was
deflecting attention from herself because she hadn't done
her duty on the night, but I was worried because every time
it hits the press that a police officer isn't doing their job properly, another victim will decide not to trust the police. I also
didn't want to get into a "she said / she said" slanging match
in front of the jury, where counsel play the two of us off
against each other. The only time the jury gets to see you is
when you are in the witness box and they make up their
minds quite quickly as to whether you are a credible person.
Having two women say nasty things about each other might

be good entertainment for the media, but it wasn't good for the case.

My day came. Mr Lederman was his usual bully boy self, trying his best to make me look like a liar. The thrust of both his and Mr Grunwald's assertions was that I had already made my mind up about the guilt of the defendants and was therefore just making the facts fit my theory so I could close the case. If that was all they had, I was in for an easy time.

I had already been asked many times in the witness box whether I was under pressure to solve a case. I guess the answer is yes, but not in the way the questioners were implying. We are under pressure because a murderer is at large and may harm someone else. What really drives us is the fact that someone has lost their life and, in most cases, a family has been torn apart by grief. That isn't the kind of pressure that makes you charge someone just to say you have solved it, it is the kind of pressure that makes you want to find the person responsible and bring some measure of justice and closure for the family.

A huge amount of resources go into every murder investigation. It is the most serious crime we deal with other than terrorism, which is, in effect, mass murder. That is one of the reasons that most murders are solved within the first two weeks. However, that does not mean the investigation is rushed. One of the many positive outcomes of the Macpherson inquiry into the botched initial investigation into the murder of Stephen Lawrence was the professionalisation of murder investigation. In addition to specialised training, that professionalisation now includes the recording of every decision. Any murder that is unsolved within forty-eight hours is reviewed by a detective superintendent. Anything still unsolved after twenty-eight days undergoes a complete head-to-toe review by an independent team of highly experienced detectives. It is their job to challenge the investigation, to double-check and to find what the senior investigating officer has missed.

Charging a suspect is the decision of the Crown Prosecution Service, not the police. They are an entirely independent body from the police and they pride themselves on that independence. There are two tests to be satisfied: public interest and evidential sufficiency. Let me assure you, they scrutinise every scrap of evidence. There is absolutely no sense of a charge being a foregone conclusion. The police are obliged by law to reveal to the CPS anything that undermines the prosecution or assists the defence. All in all, there are so many checks and balances in place within our criminal investigation process that the chances of a completely innocent person being charged with murder, much less convicted, are remote indeed.

I am always happy, therefore, to field that particular question. I explained that I wasn't trying to build a case against Mahmod when I spoke to the officer – I was trying to find out what had happened to Banaz. Mahmod was a suspect, but so were numerous others at that stage. I was open minded and if I could have eliminated him from the inquiry I would have. I had, after all, eliminated numerous other men, including Banaz's ex-husband. All I had wanted was to establish the facts so I knew whether Banaz was a witness of truth, whether she was credible.

The jury started questioning me. I mean directly questioning me while I was in the witness box. I had never seen or experienced anything like it. They started off by sending the judge a note, but when I answered that first question, they just called out another. It felt good to be able to answer them. Because my character had been called into question, I was able to give evidence of my good character. I read out my last three annual appraisals, each completed by a different manager. Every one of the appraisals was outstanding and there were some very gratifying comments in there. It was excruciatingly embarrassing to read them out, to be sure, but it helped to redress the balance. The DPS were in court to hear my evidence. Suffice to say it was so obvious the allegation against me was false that I was never formally investigated. They had heard everything they needed in the courtroom.

THE VERDICT

Central Criminal Court, 11 June 2007

Now all we could do was wait for the verdict. It is the point that every murder detective both loves and hates. It wasn't about the hours and effort put in, nor about personal or professional pride. It wasn't about the hundreds of thousands of pounds spent on the investigation. The outcome of this case could affect the lives of hundreds of women across the UK. If we were to succeed, it would send a clear message that the police *do* understand these issues, that we *do* have the ability to keep our witnesses safe, that we *do* have the capability and the commitment to bring offenders to justice. If we were to fail, it would simply reinforce a widely held view that the police do not care about ethnic minority communities, and that the men who rule some of those communities are invincible and nobody has the power to stop them from doing as they please – not even New Scotland Yard.

I cared more about this case than I can put into words. What had happened to a beautiful, innocent young woman was an evil crime, a terrible betrayal and an offence to every value I hold dear. Moreover, it was a murder that had arisen partly out of police failures. In my mind, there was more than one injustice to be redressed here. I had lived and breathed and slept this case. I have never cared about another case this much in my whole professional life. I badly wanted to bring those cowardly killers to justice.

Any detective will tell you that you can't second-guess juries, but it doesn't stop you trying. You can't help it. You sit in the canteen at the Old Bailey, sometimes for days on end, with your stomach turning somersaults every time the tannoy goes, trying to anticipate what is going on in the jury room. Coming back quickly can be a good thing or a bad thing. The longer you wait, the more spirits sink and the smugger the defence lawyers look when you pass them in the corridor. We console ourselves by commenting wisely about the complexity of the case and the number of charges the jury has to consider. We tell jokes to pass the time, gossip about people at work, take the mickey out of each other, anything rather than contemplate the unthinkable – that these guilty people are going to literally get away with murder. For, make no mistake about it, if you've got to this point, every officer wholeheartedly believes that the people in the dock are guilty.

Eventually the tannoy calls you back to court for the verdict, for the moment of truth, and the agony is almost over. By that time your nerves are like piano wire. There's another thing that detectives usually agree on, and that is that juries do not look at the defendants if they are going to find them guilty. They come into court and stare straight ahead of them as if abrogating themselves of any responsibility of what is about to follow. I don't blame them. These are ordinary members of the public charged with an onerous public duty. They have had to listen to weeks of gruelling and complicated evidence, some of which may haunt them all of their days. Then they have to decide on guilt or innocence – a decision which will have a profound effect on the defend-ant for the rest of their life.

We filed back in and took our seats. My heart was bang-ing away in my ribcage, fit to burst. I offered up a prayer: Please God, don't let them get away with this. Please God, Please God, Please God, over and over. I didn't look at the team, but I could feel them around me and knew they were all going through the same thing. I heard the door to the court close behind me and turned round to see who else had come in. More press most likely.

It was my detective superintendent, Simon Morgan, come to see the verdict. Perfect timing. He slid into the seat behind me and put his hand on my shoulder without saying a single word. How much that small gesture meant to me he will never know. From his own experience, he knew what I would be going through at that moment. I joked with him later that he must have heard I would be buying the beers, but I truly appreciated his support and friendship at that moment.

The jury found Darbaz Rasul not guilty of perverting the course of justice. His defence that he was threatened by Omar was accepted by the jury. I shed no real tears over this – he had already served a year in prison by the time the trial was concluded. Pshtwon Hama Khader, who pleaded guilty to the same offence, was only sentenced to time served, so there was no real difference between the two.

The jury unanimously found Ari Mahmod and Mahmod Mahmod guilty of murder. If I had to pick one emotion that I felt upon hearing that verdict, it would be relief. Sheer bloody relief at having brought that verdict home. Relief that they hadn't got away with it. Elation followed hot on its heels

as the reality sank in. We had won! We had achieved justice
for Banaz.

I looked over at the Mahmod brothers in the dock, something I had tried to avoid doing throughout the trial, and saw
not a single flicker of emotion in their faces. The jury
commented to the common serjeant that they thought Ari
was the main instigator. I thought back to Ari's comments
about Mahmod coming to him in October 2005 and asking
for help to kill his daughter and I disagreed to myself. Both
were equally responsible, both equally weak in my eyes.
Sentencing was deferred to July, the following month.

I couldn't wait to get round to the witness room and see
Bekhal and Rahmat. They were what it was all for, at the end
of the day, those courageous people who had risked everything to get justice for their loved one. I don't think I have
ever felt happier in my life than I did at that moment. I
opened the door to the witness room where Bekhal and
Rahmat were waiting. Bekhal fell to her knees and I threw
my arms around her. I don't think there was anyone in that
room who wasn't crying.

I had to go – the press were waiting outside the court. I
walked out the front door of the Central Criminal Court with
the tireless Paul Goddard from the CPS. Paul commented on
the complexity of the case: "The discovery of the body on 28
April [2006] was not the end of the case but the beginning of
an even more challenging phase. Witnesses required measures to assist them – telephone and technological evidence of
considerable value and complexity required detailed analysis
and reanalysis in order to reveal the truth of what happened
to Banaz and avoid the false trails that had been laid down."

I told the waiting cameras that there was no honour in
killing. "Banaz was a caring, loving young woman with the

whole of her life in front of her, and that life has been brutally cut short by the very people that should have loved her and protected her, in any terms the ultimate betrayal."

In reality, there was nothing I could have said that would have summed up that investigation. It had taken me through highs and lows I could never have imagined and tested me to the limit. I had discovered strengths I never knew I had. I walked off down Old Bailey with my team and got gloriously drunk.

The consequences of this verdict were far-reaching. A specialist unit was set up within the CPS to deal with honour-based violence. The degree of difficulty in prosecuting these offences and the need for specialist knowledge had now been recognised. The unit was headed by a lawyer named Nazir Afsul. I knew and liked Nazir, having worked with him on the unexplained death of a man in Belmarsh prison immediately before picking up this investigation. I felt that Banaz's death and the ensuing investigation were beginning to be a catalyst for change.

But, if her death was making an impact on the criminal justice system, it was also having an effect on the community. Police and women's rights organisations were receiving information and allegations that Banaz's fate was being used as a warning to other young women. One young woman was told that if she didn't do as she was told, she would be murdered just like Banaz, only this time the police would never find the body.

On 19 July 2007, a Newton hearing was heard by the common serjeant, in order to establish the extent of Mohammed Hama's participation in the murder. This is a hearing in which the judge decides the facts, based on evidence put before him or her. Sentencing would be the same day. Unusually, every single jury member came back to court to hear what Hama had to say.

Malcolm Swift QC was representing Hama. His case was that Hama had only become involved once the body had been put in the suitcase. There was no evidence of him being at Banaz's house that morning in January, in fact no evidence to incriminate him of the murder other than the words out of his own mouth. To account for the things he had said in those taped conversations, Hama fell back on the same excuse as Ari. Omar Hussain was responsible for killing Banaz; Hama was only repeating what he had heard Omar say.

The jury heard the lot. They heard those disgusting transcripts of Hama laughing with his brother (by now it had become clear that Mohammed and Alan Hama were brothers) as he described how they were slapping her and fucking her. Sadness and horror showed in their faces as they heard how Hama had put his foot on her back and pulled the cord around her neck and how he was kicking and stamping on her neck. They heard about Ari dragging the suitcase along the road and I saw another emotion pass through them, that of relief. They had got it right.

They heard about Beza being present in the house during the murder. They heard about burying the body in Birmingham and the efforts made to fix the water pipe. Things they hadn't properly understood during the trial, because we had been unable to use this material, suddenly made sense. So this was why the telephone and tracker evidence showed the Mohammeds travelling backwards and forwards from Birmingham. All was becoming clear.

The common serjeant sentenced all three men to life imprisonment. In relation to the Mahmods, he gave a minimum recommendation of twenty-three years for Ari and twenty years for Mahmod, reflecting Ari's role as the instigator. Those recommendations do not mean they will be released after those periods. They are the minimum length of service before which they will be eligible for parole. "This was a barbaric and callous crime," the common serjeant commented. "You are hard and unswerving men to whom, apparently, the respect of the community is more important than your own flesh and blood." Mohammed Hama received a recommendation of seventeen years minimum, reflecting his guilty plea. He didn't get a great deal of a reduction, pleading as he did at the last moment and only in the face of overwhelming evidence.

I was personally disappointed by the minimum tariffs, but it was pointed out to me that unless the judge grants an indeterminate or whole-life sentence, he or she has to sentence on the basis that the defendants will have some life left at the end of their time. Strict guidelines are set down for sentencing. The Mahmod brothers were already in their fifties and will be in their seventies before they are even eligible to apply for parole. They will have to acknowledge their guilt before then and show remorse for their murder. I don't think they will be out for a while yet.

The common serjeant commended the team for the quality of the investigation, something of which I am particularly proud. He also praised the bravery of Rahmat and Bekhal. Among the comments Rahmat made in his victim impact statement, he said, "Banaz and I were in love. She was the sweetest person in the world. She was my future." He told the judge that he now led a lonely life, not trusting anyone

enough to make friends and constantly looking over his
shoulder. He stated that he had tried to commit suicide on a
number of occasions. Sadly, the Mahmods were not the only
ones getting a life sentence.

I had secured my verdicts. The trial was over and the cases
against Mohammed Hama, Mahmod Mahmod and Ari
Mahmod were closed. But there was a loose end, and I
couldn't let it go.

Omar Hussain and Mohammed Ali were still at large. It
was clear from even the earliest of the taped conversations
that they had fled to Iraqi Kurdistan, but it didn't end there.
In the late summer of 2006 I had begun to receive intelligence from a number of sources that the two of them were
sitting in cafés in Kurdistan, boasting about what they had
done. I was incensed. Those two men had been granted
asylum on the pretext that their lives were in danger from the
regime in Kurdistan. Now, I am a strong supporter of the
asylum process, but once they had been given a new life in
the UK, these two men had committed the very atrocities
that they themselves claimed to be fleeing from. They were
not getting away with that. I didn't know how yet, but I vowed
to myself that I was going to get those two back to face justice
in the UK.

Brent Hyatt offered his services to assist with the extradition request and I gratefully accepted. But when we caught
up on the phone, he was spitting feathers. He had been in
contact with the lawyer for the CPS extradition team, who
had started off by saying it was a matter for lawyers, nothing
to do with police officers, and refused to even discuss the
case with Brent. When Brent kept pressing him, he claimed

that there was no extradition treaty with Iraq. Poppycock, frankly. Even the most rudimentary research on the internet revealed that there was a treaty. Granted, it was dated 1933 and had never been used as far as I could ascertain. World War II had happened since then, as well as two international wars and a devastating civil war, but the treaty might still be extant. The lawyer prevaricated to the point of outright dishonesty, which led us to make a formal complaint – not a position we would seek to be in with the CPS.

In June 2007, with the Mahmod brothers' trial successfully concluded, I redoubled my efforts. The next answer we were given was that the Iraqi constitution forbids the extradition of its own citizens. I couldn't argue with the veracity of that fact but was frustrated beyond belief. It was unthinkable to me that we should not at least ask the Iraqis. If we asked and they refused, at least I could put my hand on my heart and say I had tried my utmost.

My frustration was exacerbated by Brent's certainty that the Kurdistan Regional Government (KRG) would look favourably on a request from us. He had made informal enquiries on the point and been advised that the KRG thought it would be beneficial to bilateral relations if they helped us. The CPS were immovable on the subject and it looked as though we had hit a brick wall.

Then, one weekend, I received a call from the FBI. The agent was calling me from Iraqi Kurdistan to advise me that Mohammed Ali was in custody there. He had run over a young boy, driven off and left him to die. He had allegedly confessed to another man about what he had done. That man had advised him to escape to the UK, but Mohammed had told him that he had already killed someone in the UK, so that was not an option.

Now, Mohammed had paid the boy's family a sum of money, as is the custom in Iraq. The family were content with their compensation and so, as far as the death of the boy was concerned, the case was finished and Mohammed was free to leave. However, somehow – and the agent didn't know how – the judge had got wind of the fact that Mohammed was wanted for murder in the UK. He had asked the FBI to make enquiries with the British and ascertain whether we wanted him back.

Want him back? Oh God, yes please. I recounted the reluctance of the CPS to request extradition since it was contrary to the Iraqi constitution. The FBI agent was confident that the Iraqis had the power to override, or make exceptions to such a ruling. He told me that the judge was going to keep Mohammed in custody until the position was clarified. I made it clear that I had no power to make any such request and queried whether it was lawful for the judge to detain him while I made the necessary enquiries. "Yes, ma'am," came the reply.

This time I requested a face-to-face meeting with the CPS extradition seniors and asked my commander, Dave Johnston, to put his weight behind the request. Brent also attended that meeting and between us we tried just about every argument we could think of as to why we should be asking for extradition. Brent pointed out that the UK had even applied to Russia for extradition in relation to the murder of Alexander Litvinenko earlier that year. But the CPS was having none of it. By the time of this meeting, Brent was also getting enquiries from the Kurds, annoyed about the fact we were *not* seeking extradition. It was making them look bad. Still the CPS lawyer in charge of the department would not be moved: "Officer, the decision is mine to make and I am not going to make that request." But as they started filing out of the room, another (slightly more helpful) lawyer threw a comment over his shoulder. "Officer, you prove to me it's lawful and we'll make the application."

If ever there was a red rag to a bull, that was it. I started out by going to see the legal departments of both the Home Office and Foreign and Commonwealth Office (FCO). Both were firmly of the view that we should be making the application. Brent and I then took independent legal advice and went to see a barrister who specialised in extradition. We explained the problem. He, too, was firmly of the opinion that we should be making the application. With his assistance, we made representations to the CPS that Rahmat and Bekhal would seek a judicial review if the CPS refused to make the request.

Diana Nammi, who had been campaigning all this time to see "Justice for Banaz", began to lobby the Kurdish government. Articles began to appear in the Kurdish and British media, criticising the Kurdish government for not extraditing Mohammed Ali. In a *Guardian* article in November 2007, a KRG spokesperson responded:

> The British CPS wired the KRG and asked for the fingerprints of the person who had been arrested but there has been no extradition request. It is a concern for the ministry. We have asked for the arrest of the second suspect wanted in connection with the crime. The KRG want suspected criminals to face justice and if the British Government ask for them to be extradited, properly and officially, we will extradite them.

Soon, both the president and the prime minister of the KRG had spoken publicly about the matter and Mrs Hero Talabani, wife of the then president of Iraq, had shown a personal interest. At the instigation of Jasvinder Sanghera, chief executive of Karma Nirvana, a charity that supports victims of honour-based abuse, questions were asked in the House of Commons as to why we were not seeking extradition. Solicitor General Vera Baird acknowledged that the UK was a party to an extradition treaty with Iraq. But still the CPS demurred, falling back on the advice they had given in June.

I don't like being told that something can't be done just because it has never been done before. Armed with our new legal advice we called another meeting with the CPS. This time, I persuaded the lawyers from the Home Office and the FCO to attend and was accompanied again by Dave Johnston. Between the threat of judicial review, the media attention, the questions in the Commons and the legal opinions of two government departments, the CPS finally agreed to request an extradition. I floated out of the room.

The lawyer allocated to the case was a woman called Tina Whybrow. She called me on the telephone to discuss the matter. "I know how passionate you are to get these people back," she said, "but extradition is a matter between governments. We absolutely cannot be seen to be influencing the Iraqis at all in their decision and you must, at all costs, resist the temptation to interfere. *Keep your fingers out.*"

Tina seemed totally genuine and the last thing I wanted to do was screw anything up at this stage. I abided by her advice. Depositions were sworn and papers winged their way to Iraq in the diplomatic bag. All I could do was wait.

LOOSE ENDS

London, 2008

In the meantime, further evidence had become available about Dana Amin, the man who had driven Banaz's body to Birmingham. I hadn't given up on prosecuting him, either. The data from his mobile phone showed that it, too, had been used in Birmingham to call the other suspects over the relevant period. Furthermore, it had been used to phone his wife, whom he had left behind in the UK while he was in Kurdistan. In order to anticipate any claim that Dana had loaned his phone to a friend, we took a statement from his wife confirming that nobody had ever called her on that phone except Dana. The case against him was getting stronger.

We had already had the boot lining of his Lexus examined for forensic evidence, to no avail – as we knew, the vehicle had been valeted. Now we resubmitted the samples taken from the exterior of the suitcase. Bingo! This time we recovered a number of fibres that appeared to match the boot lining of Dana's car. It was only moderate in strength, evidentially, but was another brick in the wall.

Stuart Reeves, Craigy and I regularly knocked on the doors of Dana's associates and searched addresses looking for him, leaving our contact details and making sure nobody felt comfortable harbouring him. It was a kind of scorched-earth policy. We might not have enough evidence to apply for an extradition warrant in his case, but we were confident he would come back. Everything we were hearing from the secretly taped conversations suggested he was too soft and spoiled by UK living to stay in Kurdistan long term. He'd be back, and we would be waiting for him.

In January 2008 I moved out east to Barking on promotion to detective chief inspector. I had been so keen to stay on the Homicide Command, particularly as I was still hunting for Omar Hussain and Mohammed Ali, that I had deferred my promotion until there was a vacancy for senior investigating officer on the Command. Operation Baidland was only half achieved, as far as I was concerned. It was a wrench to leave my old team behind, but my new team were also excellent and, as I picked a job up on my first night there, I didn't have time to mourn.

As soon as the first trial had finished, I had started providing awareness training about honour-based violence to police officers the length and breadth of the country. I didn't want anyone else to die through police ignorance and if there was anything I could share from my own investigation, I was only too happy to do so. I taught first responders, detectives, SIOs, family liaison officers and forensic experts, among others. Before long I was teaching doctors, nurses, health visitors, midwives, teachers, social workers – pretty much anyone I thought was likely to come into contact with potential victims. As Brent Hyatt memorably put it, "You may only get one chance to save a life."

Two other things happened that summer of 2008. The first was the trial of two Kurdish men who had been living at 86 Alexandra Road at the time Banaz was buried there. One, Amir Abass, was charged with conspiracy to murder and the other, Dashti Babakir, was charged with perverting the course of justice. We didn't have any difficulty in proving that they were resident in and had control of the premises at the time. What we did have a problem with was proving that they knew the girl was buried in their back garden. As all the circumstantial evidence was weighed up, the defence made a successful half-time application to dismiss the case at the conclusion of the prosecution case. I have never been one of those officers who is sanguine about defeat. It was a massive disappointment.

The second thing that happened was truly bizarre. I was sitting in my office at Barking when I received an e-mail advising me that a Kurdish woman had made a historical allegation of rape against Rahmat.

Not once, in all the months of investigation, the interviews, the taped conversations, the multiple attempts to discredit Rahmat, had there been any suggestion that he had raped anyone. I had not even been aware that this woman knew him.

It is the policy of the Metropolitan Police to believe all of our rape victims until there is evidence to prove otherwise, but I recognised this allegation for the tactical lie that it was. This was an attempt to discredit Rahmat in order to launch an appeal against the conviction. Everyone else had tried to do so without success, but this woman had not given evidence at the trial and was therefore, potentially, a significant new witness. All she needed was a reason why she had not come forward earlier. I telephoned the appeals section at the

Central Criminal Court and asked them to keep an eye out for the inevitable appeal. Sure enough, a very short time later, Mahmod appealed against his conviction.

The Sapphire Team, who are responsible for investigating rape and serious sexual assaults, allowed me to watch a copy of the woman's interview. She was horribly convincing. If I had not known the circumstances of the case, I would certainly have found her believable. Her story was that before Banaz went missing, Rahmat had called on her unexpectedly at home and raped her in her bedroom. The reason she gave for not reporting it before was that he had threatened her that he would kill her if she told anyone. He had allegedly sent her a photo of herself in a state of undress and threatened to show it to her family if she said anything bad about him.

By rights my old team should have dealt with the appeal – the case usually stays with the team that investigated it. I was up to my eyeballs in murders over in east London. One teenager after another was being killed in internecine gang wars, all of which are very resource intensive to investigate owing to the number of suspects involved. I needed someone who understood the case to help me go through all the material in our investigation in order to disprove the allegation and withstand the appeal.

I called Rick Murphy and asked if I could borrow one of the detective sergeants for a week or two. Rick was dealing with a high-profile fatal fire and couldn't spare anyone. I was not impressed, but had no option but to crack on by myself. Every night for weeks I sat in my office, after spending the day dealing with Barking murders, trawling through the material, reading and rereading the various accounts and transcripts, comparing our evidence against the complainant's account.

My journey to work was at least two hours each way in vile traffic. There were many nights I simply didn't bother to go home, but slept at my desk.

Rahmat was spoken to in accordance with advice from the CPS. Once again, the poor man had to be dragged to London for a meeting – we didn't know where he was living except that it was at least four hours away. He was horrified at the allegation and vehemently denied ever having had unsupervised contact with the woman or having seen so much as her bare wrist. He was disappointed in the woman, as he had liked what very little he knew about her, but thought her family had probably put her up to it.

The rape was classified as a "no crime", there being evidence which proved it to be untrue, but the appeal still went ahead. I compiled a sixty-page statement, explaining the case and the scale of the ongoing attempt to pervert the course of justice. The appeal took place at the Royal Courts of Justice in the Strand. Rick came along for support. Both of us wondered whether the woman might have been put under pressure from her family to make the appeal and how it would affect her safety if she was unsuccessful, but we had no way of knowing.

The woman's barrister opened by attacking the statement that I had compiled, commenting that it was full of hearsay and opinion. The judges tended to agree and were scathing. I got the withering stare over the top of the glasses and wondered where this was all going. The woman got in the witness box and lied her heart out. It was an award-winning performance, barely a dry eye in the house. Once again I was sitting behind Victor Temple and Bobbie Cheema, firing one note after another at them to counter the false allegations. There wasn't a single point I couldn't disprove. As the day wore on the woman began to lose her cool, raising her voice.

I gave evidence about the history of the investigation and the conspiracy by the community to pervert the course of justice. I saw one of the judges look at me with renewed interest by the time I had finished giving evidence. The appeal was dismissed out of hand. Unusually, the judges commented on the woman's blatant dishonesty. There would be no further appeals.

Meanwhile, I continued to provide training for other force areas around the country whenever I got the opportunity. One day, after talking to officers in Northampton, I received an e-mail from the officer who had organised the training day. He said that the very next day, a woman had come into a police station asking for help. It was an honour-based abuse case and they had been able to understand the situation and put measures in place to help her, purely on the basis of the training I had provided. I was so touched that something positive, at least, had resulted. With the recent attempts to unravel our convictions, I had needed a boost.

Nor were they the only police who had learned lessons as a result of this investigation. One of the other teams at Barking had previously investigated the murder of a young woman called Tulay Goren. Her father was suspected of killing her for going out with a boy he disapproved of. The CPS had declined to charge on the basis of evidential insufficiency. The senior investigating officer for Tulay's case asked me to conduct a peer review, where one SIO reviews the investigation of another. I was able to point out matters in that case which had not been considered relevant by police or the CPS at the time, not least the family meeting to decide her fate. Damaris Lakin from the CPS reviewed the material with fresh eyes after Banaz's case and authorised Tulay's father and uncle to be charged with her murder. Her father has since been convicted.

The political situation in Iraq is complex and it is not, therefore, surprising that our application for extradition took rather a long time to be processed. Indeed, it seemed to me as though our request had disappeared into a black hole. I had heard that corruption was endemic in Iraq and assumed the worst. Many months passed before I heard some positive news. The government of Iraq had agreed that it was constitutional to extradite Mohammed Ali in principle, but had passed the matter to the Kurdistan Regional Government in Erbil to decide whether it would actually happen in practice.

In spite of what had been said in the media, there was absolutely no guarantee that the KRG would extradite Mohammed Ali. They are a semi-autonomous government and fiercely proud of their independence. Many more months passed with no news until one day I received an e-mail from Beverly Simpson, the deputy consul general from the consulate in Erbil. Not only had the KRG agreed that the extradition would be lawful and constitutional, they had passed the matter to the court in Sulaymaniyah for hearing. Beverly had hastily acquired a lawyer and attended court to make the formal request. She had to return the following week to get the verdict. There was no way of knowing, she said, which way the judge was leaning. Brent Hyatt was concerned about the fact that the KRG was based in Erbil, which was ruled by one political party, while the court was based in Sulaymaniyah, which was ruled by a different party. It was feasible that the court would refuse the extradition as a show of power.

That week seemed to take forever. Eventually I got the e-mail I had been waiting for. The judge had granted the extradition. We were about to make legal history and achieve the first-ever extradition from Iraq. The Metropolitan Police Extradition Unit agreed to go and collect Mohammed. There are no direct flights to Iraqi Kurdistan and none of the carriers were willing to take him on board. We therefore had to hire a jet to collect him and arrange an airfield to receive him. Routes had to be carefully worked out so that the plane did not stop anywhere on the way back where he could claim asylum. The quote came in from the aircraft company at about £20,000 – not a cheque I was allowed to write myself.

By this time, the whole senior management team had changed and nobody was familiar with the case. I went to my new boss, Vic Rae, and explained the situation. Vic was sympathetic and passed me up the food chain to Detective Chief Superintendent Hamish Campbell. Hamish had been an SIO himself and understood why it was important to me, so he passed me further up, to the commander of the Homicide and Serious Crime Command, Simon Foy. I went through the story yet again and, after hearing everything that had led to the extradition, Simon authorised the payment.

The little plane took off in December 2008 to collect Mohammed Ali. I spent a couple of days at Lewisham police station, waiting for the call to say that the Extradition Unit was on its way home. When I did get the call, it was not what I was expecting.

"Really sorry," the officer said. "There has been a hitch and they are now refusing to let us have him. We can't even land in Iraq."

There was nothing that could be done about it. They had to turn that plane around on the apron at Cyprus and come home.

I picked up the phone to Hamish to give him the bad news. He was pretty good about it – it couldn't be helped. We could not discover what that last-minute hitch was. A report in the Kurdish media suggested that the KRG blamed the central government for interference. (Later, we found out that it was the KRG who were refusing to extradite Ali, quoting the constitution as their reason.) Whatever the obstacle was, a few weeks later it suddenly got cleared and everything was on again! I gave Hamish whatever reassurances I could that this time all would be well. We handed over another £20,000 and the Extradition Unit set off once more.

On 29 June 2009 in the late afternoon, I stood with Rick, Craigy and Big Stu at a little country airport, watching the sky. My stomach was turning somersaults. In the far distance, a light appeared and I was given the nod from the ground crew that this was our man. Closer and closer the little plane came until it finally touched down and taxied to a standstill. The door opened and out stepped the Extradition Unit officer. Behind him, in handcuffs, slowly emerged Mohammed Ali.

We had done it, we had brought him home. It is difficult to articulate the feeling of satisfaction I had, knowing we had achieved this, but I have to tell you, it felt pretty good. Big Stu leaned in to arrest Ali and give him the police caution. Now all we had to do was convict him.

ERBIL

January 2010

In early 2010 I moved back to Lewisham, where I took over a third homicide team. The commute to Barking had been punishing and when a position became available at Lewisham, my senior officers kindly allowed me to return south of the Thames. It meant taking over a dozen or so ongoing cases, as well as picking up new investigations, but I was still determined to bring all of Banaz's murderers to justice.

To achieve Mohammed Ali's extradition was a monumental achievement, but it bothered me that we hadn't managed to arrest Omar Hussain. I needed to try them both together. With three already convicted of the murder and one yet to be apprehended, I was worried that the piecemeal evidence against Ali would be difficult for a jury to understand. To get Ali back and then have him found not guilty was unconscionable.

The official information I was getting back from Kurdistan was that Omar couldn't be found. Arrest enquiries had proved negative and the authorities were being advised that he had gone over the border into Iran. But details from the recorded conversations and from live intelligence sources suggested that he was living with a brother in Ranya, a small town in the hills about 50 miles from Sulaymaniyah. I didn't just find out the name of the town – I knew the vehicle he was using and even where he played pool. Rahmat had told me that Omar was a member of a powerful tribe who were protecting him. Omar had a brother in the Peshmerga, Kurdistan's military forces, and another in the infamous Asayish, their intelligence agency. I had no idea how I was going to get hold of him.

Then, in December 2009, I got the best Christmas present ever. The British consul general in Erbil sent me an e-mail to say that Omar Hussain had been shot in the thigh by one of his brothers with an AK-47 in an argument over one of their wives. His femur had been shattered and he had ended up in a hospital in Sulaymaniyah and had been arrested. Around the same time, the CPS asked me and Stuart to go to Iraq to clear up an ambiguity that had arisen during the disclosure exercise. It was only one detail in an e-mail from the lawyer in Erbil to the deputy consul general which needed clarification, but every detail matters.

So early in the New Year, Big Stu and I undertook what is known as HEAT – hostile environment awareness training. We learned how to work with close protection teams, how to spot improvised explosive devices (IEDs), how to cross deck between armoured vehicles under fire, how to deal with trauma injuries and a plethora of other useful things. A couple of weeks later, we boarded an early morning flight bound for Erbil, via Vienna. The close protection team who provide security for the consulate met us at the airport at Erbil. I had told them they wouldn't miss us: one huge man, one small woman.

We stared out of the window of our armoured vehicle as we drove to the Khanzad Hotel, where the consulate was based. So many things that we had heard in those recordings began to make sense. We passed a single-storey row of shops at least a mile long, made of cinder blocks. The thing that struck me about them was the car spares piled high on the flat roofs the whole length of the row. It was a giant breaker's yard.

Suddenly, details from the case that had seemed nonsensical began to take on new meaning. Ari's unbelievable excuse that Mohammed Hama had gone off to buy spare parts for his rental Ford Focus. Mahmod, too – his first alibi had been that he was out looking for breakers' yards. It was a pretty strange claim in this day and age in south London, but an everyday occurrence here, where there was less of a throwaway culture. It also explained Dana Amin's pride about his Lexus. There was very little infrastructure – no railways or other public transport – so if you didn't have a vehicle you would have a hard job getting around. It turned out there wasn't even a postal service. No wonder the extradition had taken such a long time!

The consulate occupied two floors of the Khanzad Hotel, which stands atop a huge hill in a mountainous region, 13 miles north east of Erbil. We were met by Beverly Simpson and given a security briefing by the close protection team. They told us that if the alarm sounded in the night we were to get dressed and sit on the end of the bed. They would come and get us. It didn't seem likely and we had been travelling the best part of twenty-four hours, so I quickly fell into a deep, dreamless sleep.

In the early hours, I was awoken by an almighty bang. What the heck was that? My heart was pounding. Was it an explosion? What was going on? I tried to put the light on – nothing. The electricity was out. No alarm was sounding, but

I got myself dressed just in case and sat there on the end of the bed like a lemon. I tried to look out of the window but could see absolutely nothing in the pitch black. I opened the balcony door to find we were in the middle of the most ferocious storm I have ever encountered. The wind was phenomenal. I got undressed and went back to bed.

In the morning, the grounds of the hotel looked like a tornado had passed over them. Small buildings had been completely demolished and I realised what the bang had been. A huge sheet of corrugated iron had been picked up by the wind and smashed into my bedroom window. Stuart and I went for a walk in the grounds of the hotel. The close protection team told us to beware of camel spiders. I thought they were having a laugh at my expense – they were all ex-military and, like police officers, like to wind each other up. It's a good thing that no one showed me a photo until later, because I have a phobia of spiders, and these are horrible. They are the size of a small dustbin lid with two sets of pincer-like jaws. Even thinking about them makes me shudder.

The Kurdish lawyer turned out to be a charming man who had driven three hours from Sulaymaniyah to see us. The ambiguity that the CPS were concerned about was quickly resolved and turned out to be a matter of language differences. In talking to him, I began to understand more about the process itself and why it had been so difficult. Out of fear of retribution, the lawyer had not been present in the courtroom, but had been to see the judge in his chambers. It spoke volumes that it was too dangerous for a lawyer to go into a courtroom.

Back in London, I pressed to get Omar back as quickly as possible so that he could be tried at the same time as Mohammed Ali. Now that the precedent for extradition had been set, the process was progressing far more quickly, but I had been unable to get Ali's criminal trial at the Old Bailey deferred because I was not able to give a precise date when Omar was coming home. I had received word that Omar had made an appearance at the Sulaymaniyah courthouse. The general consensus was that he was being well looked after in prison, was heavily protected by powerful tribesmen and was unlikely to ever be extradited. Time was now running out again.

Then, in March, I heard from Chris Bowers, the new consul general in Erbil. Bad news. The judge in the extradition case was going to dismiss the case. Omar was claiming two things: firstly, that it was a case of mistaken identity, and he was not the Omar Hussain I was looking for; secondly, he was going to produce a number of men from his powerful tribe to say that he was attending a wedding in Iraq on the day Banaz was murdered, and wasn't even in the UK. On the basis of that, the judge was going to dismiss the case. He had remanded the case for one week. This was everything I had feared.

I tried to get on the next available flight, but, maddeningly, there were no flights to Kurdistan because it was election week. The security situation there had escalated severely. Explosions were commonplace as the various parties tried to secure their power bases. Buildings were sandbagged and roads and airports closed. There was just no way of getting out there. I was ripping my hair out in frustration. Towards the end of the week, the flight ban was lifted and Stuart and I were on the first plane out to Erbil. I was not going to go down without a fight.

*   *   *

We rose early the following morning and set off from the Khanzad Hotel for the old courthouse in Sulaymaniyah in armoured vehicles, Big Stu in one, me in another – splitting the risk apparently. The journey took us through beautiful sunlit mountains, so different from the Iraq you see on the television. The close protection team were bristling with weapons and constantly scanning the surroundings for danger. It was perfect ambush country with rocks either side of the road that could have concealed a small army. The protection team pointed out objects that they said were often used as markers to detonate IEDs. I began to appreciate the effort Beverly Simpson had been through to achieve Mohammed Ali's extradition – it wasn't exactly down the road.

We attracted stares as we drove through the little villages. Small children were delighted, everyone else less so. I didn't see a single woman. Here was a mosque made of cinder blocks with a crude arrow pointing to one corner – Mecca this way. There a barrowful of fat fresh fish, bug eyed and full lipped, like illustrations from a children's book. We passed piles of rocks bearing spray-painted messages that advised us we were passing from the territory of one political party to the next, and men washing their cars in a shallow river bed. A wedding celebration was taking place in the layby of a busy main road. Men danced with men while the women sat on plastic chairs. I wondered at the fate of that bride and ached for little Banaz with her aspirations to be a mother. I pictured her meeting her husband for the first time on her father's allotment, not knowing the fate that awaited her.

As we reached the outskirts of Sulaymaniyah, one of the protection team advised me that we would be joined by a police escort, as if we were not obtrusive enough in armoured vehicles with IED bafflers on the roof. We drew up, klaxons

wailing, by an old building outside which were gathered a
multitude of men in traditional dress. Everyone turned to see
what the commotion was as our noisy convoy came to a halt
at the kerbside. Men were jostling for position, waiting to see
who had arrived. One of the close protection team opened
my door and out I stepped into the sunlight – little me. The
astonishment was palpable, but the mood quickly changed
from surprise to hostility. The crowd was made up of Omar's
tribe, who had come to the court that morning to give him
the alibi. I glanced to my right and saw Stuart getting out of
his vehicle. Time to go, girl. Head up. Walk. We pushed
forward through the crowd and into the court building itself.

Nowadays I hear they have a new court building in
Sulaymaniyah, but the old one was like nothing I had ever
experienced before. It was chaos. There were people shout-
ing, prisoners being dragged about in handcuffs, Kalashnikovs
everywhere. Coming from a society where they are forbidden
by law, one of the things that strikes you most about Iraq is
the sheer number of weapons. The place was filthy. Everything
was covered in a layer of red dust. You could feel it in your
mouth and nose. We walked up several flights of crumbling
stairs, past an elderly man who was carrying a huge old-
fashioned air conditioning unit on his back.

We were taken in to meet the judge dealing with the
extradition case. While this would never happen in the UK,
it was apparently required in Iraq. I had heard through the
grapevine that Omar's family had threatened the judge that if
he extradited Omar he would be killed. I had also been told
that corruption was endemic in Iraq, and I didn't know
whether I would even be allowed to give evidence. Would
they give any weight to the testimony of a foreign woman?
Was it already decided?

I was pleasantly surprised to find that the judge was extremely courteous. We were shown into oversized chairs and offered refreshments. His Honour pressed a buzzer under his desk and a middle-aged man in military fatigues immediately marched into the room and performed an elaborate salute. I made a mental note to get a buzzer of my own so I could wind up Rick Murphy when I got home. The judge ordered the file to be brought before him.

As Stuart placed the relevant documents in my hand, I explained that Omar Hussain was known to Rahmat, that they had lived together in the past and there was no mistaken identity. I described a distinctive mole and a gunpowder burn under his eye. I then showed the judge the photograph taken when Omar had been arrested in the UK. A minute flicker of the eyes told me he understood I had the right guy, although he said not a word. I told the judge that I had further fingerprint evidence which proved that Omar had been arrested two days after Banaz's murder, yards from where her body had been buried. The judge thanked us for our time and said he would see us in court. That was the first indication we had that we would even get as far as the courtroom.

The courtroom itself was set up along American lines. A wooden rail at thigh height separated those involved in the proceedings from the public, who sat on benches filling half of the room. Stuart and I took a seat on the front bench while the others quickly filled with Omar's relatives. I have to say it was a distinctly uncomfortable feeling having them behind me and I wondered whether I was about to get a bullet in the back or be stabbed with one of the tribal knives they carried in their sashes. A member of the protection team was sitting at the back of the court and I just had to trust him to look out for us. I forced myself to concentrate on what I was going to say.

The judge came into court and took up position. A door opened on my right and in came Omar Hussain on his crutches, flanked by guards. By now it all felt totally surreal. Here was this guy I had only ever seen in a photograph, Omar the rapist, murderer of innocents, who had thought he was completely untouchable, and I was about to present evidence against him in a Kurdish courtroom, in front of his own tribe. I felt a moment of triumph at that.

Omar's lawyer put forward his case and, in turn, I was called forward to give evidence. There was a short delay while a decision was made whether or not I was allowed to swear on the Qur'an. Again I went through the routine of describing Omar, pointing out his mole and the powder burn and showing his photograph.

The judge was scathing towards Omar. "Clearly you are the person she is looking for."

Omar's smug grin slipped just a little and he had the grace to look sheepish. Omar then gave his account of having been in Kurdistan at the time of the offence and I countered with the forensic evidence that proved the opposite. I eyeballed Omar across the courtroom. His grin had disappeared completely. The judge did not give his judgment at that time but said he would do so the following day. Omar looked over at his family as he was led from the court. He had clearly thought he would be leaving by a different door.

I left the courtroom feeling that, whatever the outcome, I had said my piece. As I was nearing the courtroom door, I was approached by a number of women who told me they had been present. They were women's rights activists who, thanks to Diana Nammi from IKWRO, had been following the investigation in the UK and had come to this court to witness the proceedings and make it more difficult for a cover-up to take place. One of the women said she just wanted to shake my hand. She said they couldn't believe that a white woman would come all this way to achieve justice for a Kurdish girl.

I was amazed and humbled. I wanted to cry at that moment. Initially I felt disbelief that they would ever think that I would do less for a Kurdish girl than I would for an English girl, but then I began to realise how much I took for granted. How many women in the UK have no belief that there will be justice for themselves? I wish I had been able to spend more time with those wonderful women, but I was whisked away and into the waiting cars before I had the opportunity to tell them how much I admired their courage in attending court.

A few days later, back at my desk in south London, I received the news from the consul general that I had been praying for. The judge had granted the extradition. Omar was coming home.

Not long after, on 19 March 2010, I was back at that same little airfield, waiting for another small aircraft to land, this time with Brent Hyatt beside me. Once again, we had had the disappointment of returning empty-handed ourselves, but this time we knew he was on board. Omar Hussain was everything I expected him to be, arrogant and rude. In the custody suite at Lewisham he told me he had put a curse on me. He was a man with a medieval mindset, after all.

THE KNOT

Iraq, June 2010

By May, we were booking another trip to Iraq. I wanted to make local enquiries about the two defendants, to obtain their antecedent history and, most importantly, to obtain copies of the court files. Mohammed Ali had made admissions about killing Banaz. Omar Hussain had gone to the lengths of even denying his own identity. All of this would be useful to put before the jury to show the propensity of these men for violence and dishonesty, but I needed the co-operation of both the courts and the police.

I canvassed the team for volunteers and was surprised how many people didn't fancy it. I thought it was a fantastic opportunity to experience something different and looked forward to going back. Craigy, Stuart and I were givens but we needed a fourth. I chose a detective constable called Neil Thomas to come with us. He was one of the stalwarts of the team and another gritty Londoner. Neil was also good company and I was pleased to have him along. The fifth and final member of the team was Nawzad Gelly, our interpreter, a charming man with a luxuriant moustache who hailed from Kirkuk.

Andy, Neil and Nawzad had to complete their HEAT course, as Stuart and I had done before them. We couldn't resist winding them up good and proper before they went, with a made-up account of how the trainers broke into the rooms at night to stage a kidnap. They would be hooded, deprived of sleep and subjected to rough handling and inter-rogation. "Take a wedge and stick it under your door," we advised helpfully. I don't think they got much sleep that first night, waiting for the door to come crashing in.

Neil returned full of stories about Nawzad. Several of the exercises involved simulated explosions. As the first one detonated, Nawzad had taken off running. The instructor had apparently yelled at him to "get his effing arse back over here". Poor Nawzad must have been wondering if it was worth the money.

This time we were going to base ourselves in Sulaymaniyah and stay longer. As such, the embassy could not support us with accommodation or security. We hired ourselves a private security company and, in consultation with them, decided to opt for a lower-profile approach, using "soft-skinned" vehi-cles – those armoured vehicles make you stand out like a sore thumb. Mind you, other than Nawzad we didn't exactly blend in with the locals ourselves: one giant, one ginger, one bald with tattoos and body piercings, and one short woman.

The security company sent a team to meet us off the plane in Erbil – they had no trouble spotting us in the crowd. The two team leaders were a huge Serb and a wiry Scot, but the teams themselves were made up of Kurdish men and it worried the hell out of me. I had seen first-hand how the men of the Kurdish community in south London had conspired and collaborated. I didn't trust them, but I had to go with it.

The hotel chosen for us was built into a hillside. Our rooms took up the whole first-floor corridor. We were given yet another security briefing before the Serb took us individually to our rooms. The bedroom door clicked shut behind me and I was alone. As I started to check the security of the room and familiarise myself with the escape routes, a slight movement caught my eye. The net curtain had moved. I whipped it back and nearly jumped out of my skin. The sliding balcony door was open and there, standing just a couple of feet away and staring straight at me was the nastiest-looking man I have ever seen, with an AK-47 across his chest. My eyes never left his, waiting for him to make a move, unable to look away. I groped blindly to shut the balcony door, although what protection I thought this would have given me was anyone's guess. We stood there like that for a couple of seconds before realisation dawned on me. He was one of us. I closed the door and pulled the curtain.

As soon as we were showered and changed, we set to work. Almost straight away we ran into problems. Although the consul general had informed the police of our intentions, the officer we needed to speak to was now refusing to co-operate with us. Apparently, it was simply too risky to be seen to provide us with material which might aid the prosecution. Luckily, we had a mutual friend, one of the women's rights activists, who agreed to help me by inviting him out for dinner with her and her sister. He was more than a little surprised, later that evening, when the four English officers turned up unannounced and slid around the circular dinner table. But a couple of glasses of beetroot "wine" later, he agreed to come and meet us later that night.

That first meeting was held in an underground meeting room with guards on the door. The officer was clearly very nervous. He was also clearly bemused at the fact that a woman was in charge and tried his best to score points. I stifled a yawn at one point, at which he accused me of showing weakness in front of my men. I assured him that "my" men were under no misapprehension about my strength and would follow me anywhere. I was getting away with the tough act, too, until a cockroach ran over my foot and I jumped out of my seat.

So instead I decided to use his ego to my advantage and set about flattering him. God forgive me, I praised his importance, his fitness, the fit of his uniform, his moustache, his importance again. I laid it on with a trowel. Out of the corner of my eye, I could see the guys making vomiting gestures. Craigy later said he hadn't come across such bullshit since he read my last application for promotion. Harsh but fair. Anyway, it worked. The officer agreed to discuss it further, but we would have to persuade his boss.

The next day, we went to the old courthouse to see what could be done about getting the court files. We saw the same judge who had dealt with the extradition and he kindly agreed to let us take copies of the relevant documents. We were shown into an office where workers were seated three to each single desk. Most were women. I made a connection with one of them straight away as we looked at each other's shoes and smiled. Shoes are a universal language.

Photocopying those files was a laborious process for a number of reasons. Firstly, the electricity kept failing. When it did so, the air conditioning also stopped and so did everyone in the building. Quite literally, everyone just sat down quietly and waited for the electricity to come back on. The heat was like opening an oven door. The real obstacle, however, was a human one. A woman had been assigned to us to do the photocopying, although we were perfectly capable of doing it ourselves. A man approached her and said something to her. He was the living image of Ari Mahmod. Nawzad told me that the man had told the woman not to give us everything, hold things back, so we stood over that woman and watched her like a hawk. Ari lookalike clearly didn't like this and told me that I didn't have the correct authority to take copies of the files. I told him the judge had authorised it, but he was insistent. We carried on copying anyway, while he stormed off to see the judge. I told Neil to be prepared to just put the whole file in his backpack if I gave the word. I wasn't leaving without those papers.

The judge came to see us, looking embarrassed. The clerk was technically correct, he told us; we actually needed authority from the minister of the interior. No, it couldn't be done over the phone, I would have to go and see him in person in Erbil. I wasn't about to let the clerk win. Painstakingly slowly, I started to place numbered sticky notes on every page and catalogue them so that I would know if anything was removed. The clerk was incensed, trying to get me to leave the building. The angrier he got, the slower and more deliberate I got. Every time I stuck a sticky note on, I eyeballed him and told him I would hold him personally responsible if that page went missing. The atmosphere was tense, to say the least. Eventually the judge came down and asked us to leave. The court was shutting for the day.

We met our police officer friend for lunch. More grovelling. He was now warming to us and we made an appointment to see him and his boss the following morning. That gave us the afternoon to try to arrange a meeting with the minister. We left Nawzad at the hotel doing some translation while the rest of us went to the firing range for some firearms instruction, in case we had to defend ourselves in a firefight. We learned to operate just about everything from a 9mm to a belt-driven machine gun. I had never fired anything other than a shotgun previously, but I had a whale of a time. The only problem was that the recoil of the weapons badly bruised the right side of my face. I looked as though I had been in a car crash.

The minister was totally unavailable, we were told. "He is travelling." "He is busy." "We will call you back." It was clear we weren't going to get to see him. I only had a limited amount of time in the country and there was no way I would be able to persuade the boss to let me come back a fourth time. If I went home empty-handed, that was it. I laid out the situation to the security team and they played a blinder. Phone calls were made, levers pressed, people spoken to in the right places and suddenly the whole thing unlocked. Come tomorrow morning, we were told, and the minister will see you. We decided to split our resources. Craigy and I would go to Erbil to see the minister and Stuart and Neil would go to the police station to speak to the chief of police. Everything was riding on our performance the next morning.

Now, I had been determined that we wouldn't get drunk on this trip. I didn't want us to be a liability to the security team and we needed to have our wits about us. That afternoon, Stuart began making lip-smacking noises to tell me he wanted a pint. I managed to keep him busy until dinner time, so that he couldn't wander away to the bar. Then we all went to eat on the rooftop. The temperature by this time was perfect and the sky was a dusty pink. We looked across at cranes nesting between satellite dishes and aerials. The mountains loomed purple in the background. The sound of the muezzin could be heard calling people to prayer. I haven't travelled a great deal outside Europe and America, and I found it magical to experience another culture.

The booze started flowing, my good intentions went to the wall and we spent the evening doing what we do best, telling the old stories and making fun out of each other. Late in the evening Stuart thought it would be a good idea to challenge our Serbian friend to an arm wrestle. Just to spice it up, he placed lighted candles on either side of the table, so that the loser would burn their hand. Now, both were of a similar size but the Serb was like a slab of granite. He had been in the Serbian army since the age of fourteen and was meaner than a junkyard dog. Stuart wouldn't be dissuaded, not that we tried too hard. Suffice to say that it wasn't too long before he was blowing at the singed hairs on the back of his hands.

The following morning Stuart was wrecked. He had the worst hangover ever. I needed him to go to the police station and persuade the police chief to give us the background on our two defendants. He needed to be at the height of his persuasive powers and right now he couldn't even persuade himself to swallow a bit of toast. Our acerbic Scot was also the team medic, and he gave Stuart some sort of magical cure. I have no idea what it was but I wish I could patent it – it worked like a charm. But it came with a warning: you will be good as gold for a few hours, but after that you will crash hard. Time to get cracking.

In the ministry, we bumped into some of the old security team from the consulate. They were amazed to see us back in the country and were thrilled to hear about the extradition. We told our story to the minister, who graciously granted us authority to take copies of the files (without asking about the bruise on my face), and drove the three hours back across the mountains to our hotel. It was late afternoon by the time we arrived and Stuart was back in bed. Neil filled us in on their day.

I have mentioned how people take a liking to Big Stu. That morning he had been in to see the most senior officer in the region. Bear in mind that only two days previously, this man wasn't even prepared to speak to us. Within half an hour, Neil told us, Stuart and the officer were playing Jack and Rose from the movie *Titanic* and singing "My Heart Will Go On", Celine Dion style. We didn't believe a word of it. Then Neil showed us the photos. There they were, standing at the prow of an imaginary ship, grins all over their faces.

After visiting the police, they had been to the Amna Suraka Museum at the former Ba'ath Party headquarters. Outside, everything had been left just as it was when the Kurds took the building, the tanks still in position. The nasty-looking guy from outside my bedroom window had proudly pointed himself out in a photo in the museum. There he was, standing on a tank, part of the battle to take possession of the building.

Neil was clearly affected by the harrowing exhibits. In that building, thousands upon thousands of Kurds had been tortured, raped and murdered. Inside, Neil told us, 4,500 tiny lights represented the villages destroyed, while 182,000 shards of mirror represented all those Kurds massacred by Saddam's regime. Life-sized models of people showed the torture they underwent at the hands of their captors. The models were entirely white, like negatives. People were electrocuted, their feet whipped, their bodies suspended from the ceiling by their arms behind their backs. Women were confined to one room, where they slept, ate and, after being repeatedly raped by their captors, gave birth. It sounded chilling.

We returned to the court the following day and went back in front of the judge. After a short delay while the signed permission was faxed across, we returned to the office to make our photocopies. We had brought a small gift of chocolates, which the women appreciated. Ari's lookalike refused his, of course. Once again, he prevaricated, pretending the file could not be found, but eventually he brought it, we photocopied it and left.

That evening, as we were sitting around chatting before dinner, we had a surprise visitor. Stuart's new friend had come to pay us a visit. He had brought with him two boxes of Turkish delight, very much prized in that region. Middle Eastern men are much more tactile with each other than we stiff-necked Brits and this man did not disappoint us. He squeezed himself onto the bench next to Stuart and slid his hand between Stuart's thighs. I thought Stuart's eyes were going to pop out of his head, but he was very self-controlled, given the circumstances. Not content with that, the officer then suggested that he and Stuart should get a massage together and squeezed a handful of Stuart's breast. We didn't dare look at each other.

Building a good relationship with the officer had clearly paid off, for he also brought copies of Omar's and Mohammed's criminal records and gave us some important information about Omar. A very violent man from an extremely influential family, he had already riddled the local mayor's house with bullets as a warning not to aid the authorities. On another occasion, police officers were behind him when he was heading for the Iranian border on a smuggling expedition. Omar spotted the officers behind him and pulled over. As he approached the police car, Omar pulled out a huge knife and slashed the tyres so that they could not follow him.

Officers would not provide a statement about those incidents and the criminal history, while interesting, was not in a
format we could use in evidence. We asked if we could go to
the town where he had been living prior to his capture but the
officer refused. It was lawless in those hills, he explained. Too
dangerous even for police. No wonder the Mahmods felt they
were above the law – in the land of their birth, they were.

On the last evening, we took the security teams out for
dinner as a gesture of thanks for taking good care of us. In
the garden of a restaurant, we sat around long tables under
the stars, eating and chatting with the assistance of a couple
of English speakers. It felt good to be able to see the positive
side of Kurdish culture, after our experiences in London.

Back at the hotel, the Kurds had a surprise waiting for us.
Like everybody else, they loved Stuart. They were fascinated by
his size, as most Kurdish men are fairly small in stature. They
had arranged for a traditional Kurdish costume to be made to fit
him, complete with headdress, and now they started to dress
him up. He had to have a moustache. I borrowed a pen and
drew him a very thick, black moustache before realising it was
a permanent marker. He would be wearing that moustache a
long time. I was literally crying with laughter.

He stepped into the traditional trousers, which are drawn
in at the waist with a drawstring. Among all that mirth and
merriment, I watched as one of the young Kurdish lads deftly
fashioned a knot that allowed the string to be tightened or
loosened with one hand, and I sobered. I asked him to show
it to me again. I had seen that knot before. I thought back to
the taped conversations. *Mohammed made the cord like a
hook.* I could picture exactly how his fingers had moved as he
did that. *I wound the cord around her neck so tightly it was
cutting into her flesh.* I hadn't known the significance of the

knot for the first murder trial, but it could be significant for the second one.

Back in England, throughout that summer, we prepared for the forthcoming trial. We had all moved on again and by now, Rick, Andy, Stuart and I were on different teams. What was worse was that none of us were on the original team. The whole set-up at Lewisham had changed. Simon Morgan had retired. Virtually all of the DCIs had changed. The new DCI on our old team was much less supportive, and was reluctant to allow us to use any of his staff. I actually had another DCI at Lewisham tell me I should not have gone after Omar Hussain and Mohammed Ali, that I should have stopped after convicting Banaz's father and uncle. He might have been content to do half a job, but I was not.

A third man was standing trial with Omar and Mohammed. We had arrested a man by the name of Sardar Sharif Mahmod – the man we had found at Mohammed's address when we'd first searched it. We believed he had been the fourth man in the Ford Focus, and we had charged him with threatening to kill Banaz and Rahmat on 22 January 2006. Rahmat had picked him out in an identity procedure some months previously. When he was finished, the officers brought Rahmat upstairs and showed him into the CID office. He was genuinely thrilled to see us and quite emotional. He was also pleased to tell us he had picked someone out in the procedure.

"Tell me," he said, "is his name Sardar?"

We couldn't discuss the suspect or the case with him for evidential reasons, but we had a cup of tea with him, talking about safe subjects. He was obviously still struggling to come to terms with Banaz's loss, but said he was trying to find work and playing football, trying to rebuild his life.

Once again, we were taping the Mahmods' conversations in prison. Ari and Mahmod were still conspiring to pervert the course of justice, even from behind bars. Ari was trying to find another, unused witness, to give an account that Rahmat had killed Banaz and confessed to the murder. Meanwhile, Mahmod was getting Behya to provide yet another account. To explain why she hadn't come forward earlier, she would say Rahmat had met her while she was out shopping in Peckham and threatened to kill her. Mohammed Hama, for his part, had been in touch with his mother, apologising for not being able to care for her. She gave her son her blessing, called Banaz a whore and told him he had done the right thing.

As always, we wanted to present the strongest possible case to the court. We decided to interview Hama under the Serious Organised Crime and Police Act (SOCPA) 2005. One of the provisions of SOCPA was to provide direction for when a person convicted of an offence could give evidence against another person charged with a serious offence in return for a substantial reduction of their sentence. However distasteful it may seem, there are occasions when it is necessary to work with offenders in order to convict even more unsavoury offenders.

Andy Craig is a specialist in suspect interviewing, including under the auspices of SOCPA. He set about conducting what is known as a scoping interview with Hama. Hama almost snatched his arm off. "I wake up in that cell, every day," he told Andy, "and wonder how I got myself in this mess. This was none of my business, it was a family affair." He said he would tell us everything we wanted to know and happily give evidence against the others. I was looking forward to hearing what he had to say, especially as there were still so many unknowns.

Some weeks later, with the appropriate authorisation from the Crown Prosecution Service, Andy set off to interview Hama. Sadly, what he came out with in interview was a complete pack of lies. Bearing in mind that he had pleaded guilty and we had him on tape confessing to raping and strangling Banaz, he now concocted an account which sought to exonerate not only Mohammed Ali and Omar Hussain, but also himself. It was pure madness. He had clearly sat down with the transcripts of those taped conversations and the telephone evidence and manufactured a story which side-stepped all of the incriminating evidence. It was page after page of ridiculous lies.

It wasn't only that we couldn't use him as a witness – I was now duty bound to disclose both this new, fictitious account and the taped conversations. I could not use the taped conversations myself, due to their inadmissibility as hearsay. Despite this, however, they could actually be used against me if they supported Hama's account and assisted the defence. There was nothing for it, it couldn't be helped. I just had to hope the defence would form the same opinion as us about Hama's unreliability.

THE FINAL HEARING

October 2010

The trial of Omar Hussain, Mohammed Ali and Sardar Sharif Mahmod very nearly didn't happen at all. In early September 2010, I was on holiday with my family in Croatia. We were on a ferry boat, crossing over to a little island for a day outing when my mobile rang. It was Rick.

"Rahmat is refusing point blank to give evidence," he said. "His family in Iran have been threatened and he is terrified." Rick went on to say that he had arranged a meeting with Rahmat and that he and Craigy had spoken to him face to face, but he was adamant that he wasn't going to give evidence. That was a real worry. Rick got on well with Rahmat, and if he and Craigy couldn't persuade him, nobody could.

On day one of the trial I had to go and ask for a delay. Not only would Rahmat not give evidence, he wouldn't even give us a statement explaining why he couldn't give evidence – he was simply too scared. It turned out that his family had been threatened at a funeral across the border in Iraq.

"Please, Caroline," Rahmat said, "I have lost everybody in my life. Please don't make me lose these people. They are all

I have left in the world." He was pleading with me. What could be done to make them safer? I asked. Rahmat thought that if they could move to Tehran they would be safer, but they had no money to do so.

I racked my brain for a way to help. Days were passing, and although the common serjeant was understanding, the defence lawyers were champing at the bit to have the case dismissed. They pointed out to the judge that we could not even prove that a funeral had taken place, much less that the threats had been issued. We had nothing evidential to show the violent nature of these men or their families.

I dispatched Craigy and Neil back to Iraq to trace that funeral and any relatives who could give evidence about the threats. "I need it by Monday," I told them. In the meantime, I spoke with Rahmat on the phone several times a day, trying to persuade him to give evidence, without success. I rang consulates in Iraq and Iran, trying to find asylum options. You miss 100 per cent of the shots you don't take, after all.

I went to see my commander, Simon Foy, and asked him for £10,000 to move Rahmat's family. I talked him through all the various options and alternatives. He wasn't impressed, especially given that he had just spent a fortune sending Craigy and Neil back out to Iraq with another close protection team, but Simon was nothing if not a good listener. I pointed out that all the money we had spent so far on this investigation would be for nothing if the court case didn't go ahead. Amazingly, he gave me the money and I was straight on the phone to Rahmat, confident this would solve the problem. He was furious with me!

"I have never asked you for money. Do you think my family are so shameful to accept money from you? My family have farmed that land for generations, they will stand and fight to the death." Boy oh boy, had I got that one wrong.

I was all for deposing Rahmat, forcing him to come before the court. I wasn't going to let this slip away from me now, especially having achieved a minor miracle to get the last two murderers back from Kurdistan. Bobbie Cheema refused to entertain the suggestion, citing Article 2 of the European Convention on Human Rights – the right to life. If we deposed Rahmat and his family got killed, we could be held responsible. Desperate, I argued that I had offered a way of keeping them safe and it was their choice to stand and fight, but Bobbie was having none of it. She was right, of course.

Andy and Neil returned from Iraq triumphant. Not only had they traced the funeral, they had found the man who dug the grave and taken a statement from him. The gravedigger was an off-duty police officer. Apparently, it is quite common for police officers to dig graves as a way of earning overtime. Later, the Serb and the Scot had driven Andy and Neil far up into the hills above Sulaymaniyah, into that lawless territory where even their own police had been afraid to go. There they had traced the mayor whose house had been riddled with bullets. The mayor's wife made them a beautiful meal, which they shared with the mayor, sitting on a carpet in his house, and he agreed to give a statement about Omar's intimidation and violent behaviour. The faces of the defence teams were a picture when they heard the lengths we had gone to in order to obtain this evidence. The judge was less surprised, having lived through the first couple of trials with me.

The very last throw of the dice was to plead with Rahmat face to face. This may sound simple, but he was in Witness Protection and, while we didn't know where he was, we knew the journey took many hours each way. Eventually we met him in Lambeth, in an old garage there. We sat in our car, under some old railway arches. As always, Rahmat was pleased to see us, but he wouldn't budge an inch when it came to giving evidence. We talked for about half an hour. I reminded him that we had been to Iraq to get these people back and they would be free to walk out of court and live lives of free men in the UK if he didn't give evidence. We talked about the atrocious manner of Banaz's death. Nothing worked. Just as I was about to give up, I reminded him how much he had loved Banaz and how much she had loved him. It obviously touched a raw nerve, because he suddenly just capitulated. "OK, I'll do it, I'll give evidence." Thank God, thank God. I got his signature on a statement in about ten seconds flat.

Before the murder trial began, we had a hearing to determine the legality of the extradition. It was suggested that Omar had been living in Iran and that I had lured him back into Iraq, somehow, in order to have him arrested. I explained to the judge that my intelligence was actually to the contrary – Omar was being protected by his brothers, who were lying to the authorities. He had actually been living in the compound of one of those brothers, although he did frequently cross the border into Iran when he was smuggling. The extradition was ruled legal.

A couple of weeks later, I was less pleased with the way the murder trial was going. It was bitty and piecemeal and I could see the jury struggling to understand the story. I had lost a lengthy legal argument about using the Iraqi court files in evidence. Mohammed Ali claimed that anything he said in those statements about having murdered Banaz had been obtained under duress. I made numerous lengthy calls to Kurdistan, trying to persuade judges, prison officials, police officers, anyone, to come to court to prove otherwise. Nobody would come. I arranged visas, I tried to sort out live links so that evidence could be given via video. Nobody was willing to give evidence. One very senior man told me it was simply too dangerous. "I have to drive an hour and a half through the mountains to get home. I will simply be killed."

I couldn't argue with that. I was going home to my family that night; he had the right to do the same. Instead, I produced photos of Ali in custody showing there wasn't a mark on him. It wasn't enough. It was up to me to prove he hadn't been under duress, not for him to prove otherwise. The judge ruled against their use. All that work in Iraq had been for nothing. I could almost hear that clerk at the Sulaymaniyah courthouse laughing.

As anticipated, we had not been able to use the recorded conversations in evidence because they were hearsay, but we did have to disclose them to the defence because they corroborated some of the lies told by Mohammed Hama. Thankfully, nobody, neither the prosecution nor the defence, wanted to touch Hama with a barge pole because he was so very obviously telling a pack of lies. The taped conversations, therefore, simply were not used. The jury would never get to hear him describing how he, together with Omar and Mohammed Ali, had abused and strangled Banaz. They would never hear Ari explaining why she had to be killed and never hear them all calling her a whore and saying she deserved it.

Because Hama and the Mahmods had either pleaded guilty or already been found guilty, many of the facts were "agreed" by all parties outside of the courtroom. In some ways it was useful that the others had been found guilty, as it showed that the prosecution was credible, but in other ways it was less so. It can actually be harder for the jury to piece everything together, as they don't hear the first half of the argument being played out in front of them.

Rahmat gave evidence. He was doing well until he was asked about Sardar Sharif Mahmod. He then went against everything he had previously said and denied that Sardar had made any threats. Victor Temple reminded him what he had said in his statement, but Rahmat stood firm. It was infuriating but there was nothing we could do about it.

Behya, Banaz's mother, simply refused to come to court to give evidence. We ended up summonsing her and physically taking her to court. Imagine having to summons a mother to give evidence against the men who killed her daughter. Once in the witness box she backtracked on what she had written in her statement and we ended up treating her as a hostile witness. Her significant witness statement, which she had signed, was read out to her. She wriggled like a fish on a hook. She retracted everything. It was all lies made up by the police, she said. She denied saying any of it, even when it was pointed out to her that the interview was recorded. She hadn't understood, it was a language issue. No – you had an interpreter, she was told. The interpreter was in on the conspiracy, she said. Is that your signature? No, no, it's a forgery. One by one, Victor got his points in about Banaz having an appointment at the police station, about the phone call from Ari, about Banaz being at home on the morning of the 24th and never being seen alive again by anyone. But it was hard going.

Omar Hussain and Mohammed Ali each gave evidence to explain their usage of the telephones and their whereabouts, all of which were to do with collecting money for Ari Mahmod's *hawala* banking business. *Hawala* is a form of money transfer that exists outside formal banking arrangements and is therefore not subject to regulations. It is a system based on honour. It has also been used to launder funds and support illegal activity.

More cronies came forward to give false evidence on behalf of the two murderers. To my anxious eyes, the jury looked confused and disengaged. One young woman covered in tattoos didn't seem to be paying attention – I even thought she had fallen asleep on several occasions. As the jury passed me in the cavernous hallway during one of the many occasions they were asked to leave because of a legal point, I heard one woman say she was bored. Bored! All that work, all that heartache and she was bored. I could feel it slipping away from us.

But then something strange happened. Mohammed Hama sent a letter to the judge. "In the interests of justice," it said, "I must come to court and give evidence." Of course, the judge knew this case like the back of his hand by now, having lived it along with the rest of us. I can still see him reading aloud that letter and turning to the court with raised eyebrows.

"Yes, well, how do you want to deal with this?" He put it to the various counsel representing the case – did anyone want to hear what Hama had to say?

Neither the prosecution nor the teams for Omar and Mohammed Ali wanted anything to do with him, but the counsel for Sardar thought it would be beneficial to her client's case. Rahmat had already, apparently, "gone soft" on Sardar, so if she could get Hama to confirm that no threats were made, her client was pretty much home and dry.

And so, Mohammed Hama was hauled from prison and into the witness box. He told one stupid lie after another. He had been tricked into pleading guilty by his lawyer, he claimed, it was all Rahmat's fault, he had killed her. The tape recording of him saying he had raped and strangled her was all a misunderstanding. He was actually just repeating what Rahmat had confessed to him. Rahmat had collected Banaz in a van and killed her in his flat. It went on and on. We knew it was nonsense, but the jury had no knowledge of the previous trial and all the lies that were told there. I should imagine it all sounded pretty plausible to them.

Hama was furious with Andy Craig. He called him corrupt and told the jury that Andy had promised him many years off his sentence if he would only give evidence against Omar and Mohammed Ali. Put like that it sounded awful – it certainly made the jury sit up. Craigy jumped in the witness box to explain how SOCPA worked and why we didn't use Hama as a witness, namely because he could not be considered a witness of truth. It was pointed out to Andy that some of what Hama was saying could be proved. He replied that all the best lies have an element of truth to them, that's what makes them believable. I could see jury members nodding.

Hama exonerated Sardar of all blame. Then it was the turn of Anthony Heaton-Armstrong QC, representing Omar, to cross-examine him. Hama was warming nicely to his theme and started to go off brief, coming out with answers that were not consistent with his previous account. Instead of stopping at that point, Mr Heaton-Armstrong started questioning him about something that he had said in the taped conversations. Legal argument followed in which it was ruled that all of the taped conversations were now admissible. The jury were going to hear the lot!

The moment the transcripts were read out, you could see the understanding dawning on the jury. Suddenly, it all made sense – Omar and Mohammed Ali's involvement, Mohammed Hama's lies, the killing, the suitcase, everything.

Closing speeches were made and the judge summed up. We retired to the canteen and prepared for a long wait while the jury deliberated over the complexities of the evidence. Just three hours later we were called back into court. A question, we thought. No, the usher told us: a verdict.

I filed back into court with Rick, Andy, Stuart and the others. We were trying to appear nonchalant and probably failing miserably. It is highly unprofessional to show emotion during court proceedings, no matter how strongly you feel. I took a seat, smiled and nodded to the prosecution counsel. Whatever took place now would change the lives of many people in this room. I made some insouciant comment to the defence counsel as if I did this every day of the week and I opened my A4 notebook. I looked across at my team. I loved these guys. They had been with me from the first day of this investigation and we had lived through it all together. They had become a second family to me.

A loud knock on the door and in came the common serjeant. I thought how much I loved this judge and then knew for certain that I was feeling hysterical. The door to the jury room opened and in came the jury. For some reason, the tattooed woman came in first and I found myself looking past her for the middle-aged white guy I had earmarked as the jury foreman. What was going on? The young woman seated herself in the chair reserved for the foreman. Surely not? But she hadn't been paying the slightest bit of attention – had she? My stomach sank.

I risked a look at the rest of the jury. They were all seated now and almost as one they turned to look at the defendants.

Oh well, that's it then, it's all over. I didn't look around me any more – not at my colleagues, not at Victor and Bobbie, certainly not at the common serjeant. I tried to observe the jury without being obvious, a casual look at the dock, a casual look at the clock, down at my notebook, back to the jury. Time stood still.

"Would the defendants please stand."

They stood.

"Members of the jury, have you reached a verdict upon which you all agreed?"

"Yes."

"On count one, murder, do you find the defendant Mohammed Ali guilty or not guilty?"

"Guilty."

Relief, sheer bloody, glorious relief and joy flooded through my body. I wanted to jump up, shout, laugh, cry, punch the air, pull my shirt over my head, footballer style, hug my mates and thank the jury all at the same time. Of course, I did none of the above. I looked up momentarily under my eyebrows at the jury without making eye contact, then back to my notebook with great concentration, as if the most important part of this whole process, the very verdict itself, rested on me writing this one word: GUILTY.

Sardar Sharif Mahmod was found not guilty, but Omar Hussain was also found guilty of murder. He and Mohammed Ali were sentenced the following day, 11 November 2010, to life imprisonment with a minimum recommendation of twenty-three and twenty-two years respectively. The common serjeant, in sentencing, said, "You were willing and active participants in what was an agonising death and a deliberately disrespectful disposal. You are hard and callous men who were quite prepared to assist others in the killing in the so-called name of honour and who placed respect from the community above life, tolerance and understanding."

After all this, all these years of searching and lies, we had finally achieved justice, true justice, for Banaz.

It was over.

THE LAST WORD

In 2012, I was a detective superintendent working on the Counter Terrorism Command in London. I had, by now, over thirty years' service and could have retired, but was still enjoying myself. One day I had a phone call from Stuart Reeves, inviting me for a beer. He and Craigy were at Belgravia police station, just up the road. He took great delight in telling me that they were just in the process of charging Dana Amin. The fool had risked coming back to the UK and a little bird had whispered in Stuart's ear where he could be found.

By now there wasn't a single one of us left on the original team at Lewisham and the job of prosecuting Dana fell to DS Andy Nimmo. I was anxious about it being handled by someone who hadn't been part of the original team, but he did an absolutely outstanding job and Dana was convicted of perverting the course of justice and preventing the lawful burial of a corpse. His defence had been that he had loaned his car, his bank card and his mobile to a man who he knew was having an affair with his wife. Unsurprisingly, the jury weren't convinced. In December 2013 His Honour Judge Martin Beddoe sentenced him to eight years' imprisonment. In his sentencing remarks, he said, "I fear for any child you may father. I fear you are proud of the role you played and are proud to be considered a real man by your uncle [Ari] – a real man you are not."

One by one, the rest of the investigation team are retiring. Sarah Raymond, Andy Craig, Phil Adams, Simon Morgan and Rick Murphy have all retired. Children born during that investigation are now at secondary school. Craigy still has his cheeky little grin. He is now a very proud grandfather to two delightful little boys. Only Big Stu is still flying the flag. He is serving on the Metropolitan Police's Homicide and Serious Crime Command, still solving murders. We meet up occasionally for a beer or six and to reminisce. Meanwhile, Rick has gone back to work for the Met, teaching direct entry detectives how to do their jobs. It's good to know those skills aren't being lost.

Victor Temple has also retired, but Bobbie Cheema, the junior counsel I admired so much, went on to become Britain's first Asian female High Court judge. She is now Dame Bobbie Cheema-Grubb. Told you she was good!

The IPCC eventually concluded their investigation into the conduct of the officers who had dealt with Banaz in the run-up to her death. In relation to the female officer who had refused to believe Banaz, they concluded that her actions fell far below the standard which any person reporting a crime is entitled to expect. The lessons learned from her actions on New Year's Eve 2005 continue to form the basis for honour-based violence training for police officers.

In 2012, I was awarded the Queen's Policing Medal, both for leading Operation Baidland and for the work I had carried out subsequently to raise awareness about honour-based violence. It made me enormously proud to take my children to Buckingham Palace. It didn't make up for being an absent parent, but hopefully it helped them understand the importance of my absence. That medal should belong to the team of course. I always feel a bit embarrassed at receiving praise for this investigation, for it was, without doubt, the result of the most extraordinary team work.

I retired from policing in 2013. I still work to raise awareness about honour-based violence, but I miss policing every day.

In May 2016, I received a call from Rick Murphy as I was putting my groceries in the car. We hadn't spoken for some time and it was good to hear his voice. Sadly, he was ringing with bad news. Rahmat Suleimani had hanged himself and was in a coma, not expected to live. Poor Rahmat. He simply never got over Banaz's death. He never adapted to his new life, or found another love. Two days later he passed away. After everything that he had been through to achieve justice for Banaz, and all the efforts to keep him alive, he had let go of life. Rick and I were devastated. It was six years since we had seen him last and we had carried on with our own lives, but for Rahmat, there had been no moving on.

To me, Rahmat is one of two real heroes in this story. Without him, we wouldn't have known that Banaz was even missing. Her family certainly wouldn't have reported her. He risked his life to go up against his whole community and in so doing gave up everything and everyone he knew. With his passing, the world lost a truly honourable person.

And little Bekhal, that courageous young woman who risked her life to give evidence against her family? Bekhal is alive, well and happy. In 2012 the Metropolitan Police conceded that they had failed to protect Banaz and awarded Bekhal an undisclosed sum of money. I can't say too much about her as she will always be at risk, but she is thriving and has people who love her. The last time I saw her was on a hot summer's day when I met her to film an interview for Deeyah Khan's documentary, *Banaz, A Love Story*. I watched her bouncing along the pavement towards me, dressed in shorts, with a sassy haircut and a grin from ear to ear and I knew at that moment that I had won.

ACKNOWLEDGEMENTS

A few years ago I found myself driving in the pitch black and pouring rain, trying to make my way out of London. It was New Year's Eve and I was lost. I pulled into a side turning to put my glasses on and consult a map and realised, with a start, that I was in Dorset Road, Wimbledon, the scene of the attempt on Banaz's life on another New Year's Eve several years before. What an amazing coincidence. On that night of the year, one tends to assume that most people out and about are revellers, but I couldn't help wondering what dramas were taking place in the cars driving by.

I decided there and then that it was time to write this book. Enough time had gone by that I could write slightly more dispassionately about the events. I wanted to keep Banaz's name alive and not allow it to be erased as the perpetrators had wished. This is a story that needs to be told and retold, by everybody and to everybody. At least part of the reason for her death was lack of awareness on the part of professionals about honour-based violence. Telling this story helps to address that. And I also wanted to thank my team.

In a book like this, it's impossible to give everyone the credit they deserve. Homicide investigations and the subsequent prosecutions involve a huge number of hard-working professionals and this one was especially complex, involving dozens of people that I haven't mentioned. But there are a few people I want to thank personally, as we could never have achieved justice for Banaz without them.

First and foremost, there's Team 16: Detective Inspector Rick Murphy; Detective Sergeants Andy Craig, Stuart Reeve, Gary Arthur, Colin Freeman, Richard Vandenburgh and Rod Paterson; Detective Constables John Weighill, Jim Mason, Sarah Raymond, Andy Brown, Neil Thomas, Nick Stocking, Mark Randall, Clay O'Neill, Andy Mumford, Steve Martin, Claire Elliott, Laura Catterall, John Smith and Alan Hutchison; support staff Keilly McIntyre, Trish Elliott, Debbie Padwick-Taylor, Frances Beeching, Ann Raven, Lisa Roberts, Vanda Parmenter, Caroline Blackburn and Laura Andrews.

Crime Scene Manager Calvin Lawson is particularly worthy of mention. This was a case in which there were thousands of exhibits, dozens of people arrested, over fifty houses searched. Because it wasn't a conventional murder investigation, it required lateral thinking to maximise the evidential forensic opportunities. Calvin was the best crime scene manager I have ever worked with.

Without the interpreters, Ms Ali, Mr Mo and Mr Gelly, we would never have found Banaz. Working on such an inquiry carries its own risks when you yourself are from the community under investigation. Less honourable people might have been untruthful about what was on those tapes. They spent many months in a windowless room, headphones on, listening to those horrendous conversations. Thank you.

Thank you also to Peter Faulding and the team from Specialist Group International, for searching those rivers in freezing conditions.

Detective Superintendent Simon Morgan is one of the few guvnors whose opinion of me I actually cared about. His example inspired me to never give up, even when a case seemed to have gone cold. Here's an example: for many years, Simon had been investigating the case of a man who was breaking into the homes of elderly ladies and raping them. Simon had been quite badly injured on duty years earlier and was experiencing excruciating back pain as a result. Others would have retired on ill health, but he simply wouldn't go until he had solved this one job. And he got his man eventually. Late one night in October 2009, I received a text from Simon which simply said, "Got him."

For their unwavering support throughout the investigation, I thank Detective Superintendent Phil Adams, Detective Chief Superintendent Andy Murphy, Detective Chief Superintendent Hamish Campbell and Commanders Dave Johnston, Simon Foy, Sean Sawyer and Simon Bray. Also Chief Superintendent Steve Jordan of West Midlands Police, who helped me pull together that team in Birmingham. I have to say that whenever I have told this story to West Mids officers, nobody can heap enough praise on Steve Jordan, so it clearly wasn't a one-off. The man is a legend.

Detective Chief Inspector Gerry Campbell and Detective Constable Yvonne Rhoden were probably more knowledgeable about honour-based violence than anyone else in the Met. There were developments in the risk on a daily basis. They cared every bit as much as we did, nothing was too much trouble. If we needed a meeting out of hours, they were there. If we needed a surveillance team to look at someone, they were there. With so much else going on and so many other demands on my resources, it was good knowing we had such reliable partners. Gerry Campbell went on to become the Metropolitan Police's, and the de facto national, strategic lead for honour-based abuse. He retired as detective chief superintendent and still works tirelessly to raise awareness on the subject.

Damaris Lakin and Paul Goddard of the Crown Prosecution Service were outstanding. It is difficult to articulate how much work goes into preparing a case for trial at the crown court. I cannot say enough about their professionalism.

I have to say that I had a serious love thing going on for the common serjeant, Brian Barker CBE QC. Not in the schoolgirl-crush type of way, I hasten to add, more in the way you love Atticus Finch. He was a charming man, always such an absolute gentleman and always so fair. I hated some of his decisions when they didn't go my way, but he was consistent and fair – a brilliant judge.

Huge thanks to Diana Nammi from the Iranian and Kurdish Women's Rights Organisation (IKWRO), a woman with an amazing life story of her own. She has been fighting for women's rights since she was fifteen years old. At the age of seventeen she fought Saddam's forces in the hills of Kurdistan. She is now a highly influential campaigner for women's rights. Although I didn't know her story when I first met her on the gold group, or how solid an ally she was to prove, we both recognised in each other a love for Banaz and although neither of us had met her, a shared determination to achieve justice for her. She is a woman after my own heart. She continues to go from strength to strength – in 2014 she was named Barclays Woman of the Year and in 2015 she was named one of the BBC 100 Women.

The Kurdish women who witnessed Omar Hussain's trial were far more courageous than me. If anyone reading this knows those women, please tell them how much I admire them.

Jasvinder Sanghera of Karma Nirvana, a UK based charity supporting victims of honour based violence, lobbied MPs in the UK to apply for the extradition of the suspects from Kurdistan.

Southall Black Sisters gave support throughout. They know what they did.

Payzee Mahmod (formerly Payman), Banaz's younger sister, has recently started raising awareness about honour-based violence. In itself, this is an act of courage. She is an amazing young woman and I am full of admiration for her.

Thank you to Alex Christofi and Shadi Doostdar of Oneworld Publications for their patient editing and guidance and Annabel Merullo of Peters Fraser & Dunlop for helping me to tell this story.

Not a day went by that I didn't thank God for my own upbringing. My family were not well off financially, to say the least, but I was, and still am, loved unconditionally by my parents. They raised me to be independent, to have the courage of my convictions and to try to be a decent person. Their love sustained me as a child. It sustains me still.

I owe an enormous debt of gratitude to my husband and children, of whom I saw very little during this investigation. They put up with the sleepless nights, the thousand-yard stares, the falling asleep at the cinema, the missed mealtimes. Thank you.